PRINCESS AND THE PLUG 2

MZ. LADY P

NOV 2019

FR

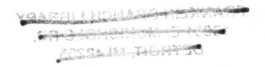

Princess and The Plug 2

Copyright © 2019 by Mz. Lady P

Published by Shan Presents
www.shanpresents.com

SUBSCRIBE

Text Shan to 22828 to stay up to date with new releases, sneak peeks, contest, and more....

SUBMISSIONS

**To submit your manuscript to Shan Presents, please
send the first three chapters and synopsis
to submissions@shanpresents.com**

PREVIOUSLY IN PRINCESS AND THE PLUG

Hercules was going to kill me when he made it home. For a whole week I had been going back and forth with myself about whether or not to confront the bitch Blanca. The more I sat up and took care of my son I became angry with myself for not fighting for my daughter. I was no longer weak ass Princess that Lucifer used to beat into submission. I was the new and improved Princess. I had a voice and a purpose. My main purpose was raising my kids and giving the life I never had. I had been sitting up resenting myself to the point that it had me angry and wanting to murder Blanca and Lucifer bitch ass.

I couldn't stop looking at the address Nurse Jones had given me. On one hand I could wait for Herc to handle the shit or I could stand up for my daughter on my own. I had already failed her at birth and I didn't want her growing up and hating me. When she got older I wanted to be able to tell her that I rescued her from the bad people.

This morning I woke up and decided that today was the day that I was going to get my daughter. Hercules telling me that he had business to take care of that would keep him out most of the day and not to wait up helped with that decision. I didn't even care if security followed me and told him about my whereabouts. I was taking a chance and going to get my fucking daughter. I'll deal with Hercules backlash later. He would be pissed at me for not telling him but even more upset about me taking one of his favorite guns. While he had been gone day in and day out I would be in his shooting gallery on the property shooting some rounds. Thank God Miami showed me what the hell to do or I would have fucked around and shot myself.

My heart sped up as I pulled up to the address which was located in a upscale subdivision. It was a good thing the front gate was open because it was definitely private property that you just couldn't get into. It wasn't a surprise that Lucifer lived somewhere like this. He had several properties that he spent his time in between. The nigga had become rich off of pussy. People wouldn't think that pussy wouldn't make a nigga millions but its very lucrative. Sadly, the human trafficking of women and kids nets traffickers billions every year. People from all over the world are paying top dollar and its sad as fuck. To have been apart of that type of industry disgusts me. It doesn't matter that I didn't do it willingly. I happened to be one of the lucky ones who was able to get away. There are still so many women and children being abused and sold into sexual servitude all over the world.

Knowing that my daughter would one day become a statistic at the hands of her father made me go even harder for her. I'll die before I allow anyone to violate her the way that I have been violated.

I took a deep breath as I got out of the car and headed towards the house. It was funny seeing the car Lucifer had originally got for me. This bitch Blanca was sad as hell to be comfortable with this man giving her all my shit. Without hesitation I rang the doorbell. I nervously tapped my feet against the pavement waiting for someone to arrive. It was just starting to get dark and I really needed these motherfuckers to answer the door so I could get my daughter and leave. It would be so good if I could get back home before Hercules made it.

"Hello, can I help you." I tried my best to control my emotions as

I stared into my daughter's eyes. A woman in a maid's uniform was holding her on her hip.

"Yes, I'm looking for Lucifer. I have a meeting with him and Blanca for work."

"Please come in. " I knew telling her that would allow me access into the house. I knew Blanca was a recruiter for him and this maid more than likely knew what they were into if she was working this close with Sophia. Lucifer would never just allow anyone onto his personal property like this. She had to be a trusted servant to even be in the same room as Sophia. I decided to take an extra step before she left the room.

"She is so beautiful. Can I hold her?"

"Oh no. Ms. Blanca doesn't like anyone touching her daughter." Calling my child that I birth Blanca's daughter enraged me. Without even thinking I pulled the gun from my pocket and pointed it at her.

"That's my daughter. Give her to me and go tell that bitch Blanca Princess is here!" I practically snatched my daughter out of her fat ass arms.

"No need for all of that Princess." Blanca said as she sauntered down the stairs smoking a cigarette.

"It's very necessary bitch! Let me get straight to the point. I'm going to walk out of that door with my daughter and there is nothing you or Lucifer can do about it."

"Take her. I don't give a fuck. I've never wanted to be her mother anyway. Hell, I never even wanted to be here with his old ass. I have no more fight in me Princess. The daily ass whooping's and brutal rapes have worn me out. Please take Sophia now before he comes home. He has every intention on grooming her to become a whore for his cause. Go Princess! Get her out of here!" Blanca was yelling and crying at the same time which made Sophia cry. I hauled ass running out of the door with my daughter she was crying and scared. My ass was crying out of joy and fear that the nigga would pop up at any minute. My fight or flight response had kicked in and I was hauling ass getting back to my car. I hated to throw her in the backseat like a rag doll but now was not the time for gentleness. Hopping inside the driver seat I took off like a speed demon out of the subdivision.

"Shhhh! Stop crying Sophia. I'm taking you home with me to a safe place. You're with your real mommy now. I'm going to take you to meet your baby brother and your step dad Hercules. You're going to love him just as much as I do." She was crying hysterically which was understandable because to her I was a complete stranger. Looking around for my phone I realized I left it at home. I wanted to call Hercules and let him know that I had Sophia and I was on my home.

"Stop crying baby! Everything is going to be okay." Sophia was in an all out tantrum and I just wanted to get her back to the house and far away from Lucifer as possible.

After driving for about thirty minutes Sophia had finally cried herself to sleep. I was about ten minutes away from the house when I spotted Hector's car on the side of the road. It looked like it had stopped so he was most likely heading towards our house. I was happy as hell to see him.

"Hey Princess! Herc know you out here?"

"No! But I'm headed to the house now before he gets there. Is something wrong with your car? Do you need a ride or something?" He leaned further in the car and I could tell he took notice of Sophia in the backseat.

"Who you got back there?"

"That's my daughter and I'm taking her home. Hercules is going to be mad that I went to Lucifer's house and got her but I needed my baby." I quickly wiped a tear from my eye that had fell.

"I guarantee you he won't be mad!" Before I could say anything Hector reached inside of the driver side window and placed a cloth over my mouth that had a strong odor on it. The anger in his eyes was the last thing I saw before I blacked out.

My head was pounding and I could barely open my eyes. It hurt that damn bad. After what seemed like forever I was able to finally focus. I started to panic as I looked around at the unfamiliar space. Thoughts of my son, my daughter, and Hercules flooded my mind. I cried remembering that Hector had done something to me. A light came on and I immediately sat up in the bed that I was lying in.

"Who are you and where the fuck is my daughter?"

"Calm down beautiful. Sophia is just fine." This older man with a strong Spanish accent pulled up a chair next to the bed I was in.

"Do you have any idea who my nigga is?" He couldn't know fucking with me.

"Yes. I do. Who doesn't know Hercules Hernandez?"

"I'm glad you do because the moment I get out of here he's going to kill you and that snake ass nigga Hector."

"I regret to inform you but Hercules is dead. So you see he won't be coming for you." I closed my eyes and tried my best to hold on the tears that was sure to fall. I didn't believe him because I didn't feel it in my heart.

"Who are you and why are you doing this?"

"These days I go by Juan Vega but Queenie knows me as Benito Delgado. Welcome home my beautiful daughter. I've missed you so much my Princess!"

ONE

PRINCESS

Staring out of the window of the room I had been being held in, I felt the urge to jump to my death. The only thing that was keeping me from doing it was my kids. I couldn't go out like that. I wiped a tear from my eye as I looked on the side of me at my baby Sophia. After two months of being with me, she has finally allowed me to love and take care of her. For the first couple of weeks of being here, she cried day in and day out. I wasn't mad though. She didn't know me for the first year of her life, so I was a stranger.

Every day I've blamed myself for everything that has happened. Had I not left out of that house to be a hero, I wouldn't be all the way in Columbia, Herc would be alive, and my son would be in my arms. The thought of my baby boy being without his parents is killing me. Day in and day out, I worry if he's being fed and changed properly. I've been thinking about Queenie as well. I'm worried if she has relapsed. Lord knows she doesn't have the mental capacity to deal with a newborn. I prayed Miami had been taking care of my son. She would love him as if he were her own. I know Bonnie and Clyde aren't doing good without Hercules. They love that man. My heart is heavy for Ziyon. How is he even managing without Bleu or Herc?

Brittani is such a daddy's girl, so I know she's going through it. These motherfuckers had no idea how much they've hurt this family. We're literally nothing without that man. This was a situation where you had to think about the good times to keep from crying.

If I had known Hector was such a snake, I would have been killed his ass. This man never gave off a bad vibe. He seemed to be down for Hercules literally, but all along, that motherfucker was a snake. Just looking at him in the backyard with Benito boils my blood. I swear I'm going to get back home to my son and make sure to kill a couple of motherfuckers in the process.

I swear I wish I could speak to Queenie to tell her the bullshit that I had learned being here. This nigga Benito is really Juan Vega. Benito was an alias he used to traffic in the states. The entire time while he and my mother ran the streets of Chicago, he was married, not to mention he has a daughter that is the same age as me. Queenie is going to lose her mind when she finds this out. All of my life she spoke so highly of him. This was definitely not the man she spoke of. I want to kill him for her my damn self. How could he do this to us?

For the first time in a long time, I wanted my mother. She had been dealt a bad ass hand, and it caused her to deal me one. I'm not justifying her actions for turning me over to Lucifer. I just feel like this nigga Benito, Juan, or whomever the fuck he is caused this shit.

I climbed in bed with my daughter and held her tight. All I could do is cry. I wanted to go home, but then again, Herc wasn't there. Closing my eyes, flashes of his car being all shot up and basically wrapped around the tree let me know he was dead. There was no way someone had survived something so horrific. Then again, my baby is like Superman. He would never let a bitch ass nigga like Hector get one up on him. My heart speaks to me, and it always has. It's telling me that Herc is not dead. I can feel him. It's a feeling I can't explain, but I just know he would never leave his kids.

"KNOCK! Knock! Can I come in for a minute?" I rolled my eyes because this damn girl Passion was getting on my last nerves.

"Come in."

"Hey, daddy wants you to come down for dinner."

"Oh, I get to eat outside of this jail cell he's keeping me in? I'm good. He can have the food sent up here to me like he's been doing."

I've been in this room for two months and all of a sudden, he wants me to sit with them and have dinner. Fuck that! I refuse to break bread with the enemy.

"Look, I know this hard for you?"

"Have you ever been kidnapped and ripped away from your newborn son?" I had to ask her this because this spoiled pampered ass bitch has never had a hard day.

"No, I haven't, but I do know he has his reasons for bringing you here. Just try to embrace us. We're family."

"Girl, your ass is smoking dick if you think we family. My family is in Chicago. Tell your father to send the food up here so that I can feed my daughter."

She knew to go ahead on about her naïve ass business. Her ass doesn't have a clue about what the hell is going on right in front of her. How could she think me being kidnapped and held against my will is okay? The more I sat in this room, the more I realized that I needed to come up with some type of plan. I have got to get home to my baby.

"You will not be disrespectful in my home!" Benito's wife Estelita bussed inside of the room and woke my baby up with her loud ass mouth.

"Girl, fuck you and this home. In case you forgot, I didn't ask to come here. A man that I don't even know kidnapped me. I don't care about this being your house. As long as I'm being held here against my will, I will never respect any of you motherfuckers."

"You got a mouth on you just like your low budget ass mother! I see why she sent you away with that rapist."

"Let's get something straight you old ass bitch! Whatever

Queenie did to me is none of your business. As a matter of fact, make that the last time you disrespect my mother. I don't give a fuck what she did to me can't nobody else disrespect her. You're so pressed about Boss Queenie. That nigga you in love with fell in love with her back in Chicago and produced me. You hate it, Estelita. Please stop walking around here like you care about me. You don't want me in your home. I'm the product of your husband's affair. It must kill you knowing your daughter and I are the same exact age, not to mention identical. One would think we were twins, but I know that's not possible."

Before she could get a word in Benito walked inside the room, and I became angrier. My daughter cried each and every time he or Hector came inside the room.

"Let me speak to my daughter please, Estelita." His accent was so thick and harsh. That bitch got the fuck out of dodge quick without so much as a word.

"I'm not coming downstairs to eat."

"You don't have to. I'll have Martha bring the food up to you. I really want to get to know you, Princess. My goal is for you to embrace the life that I'm trying to give you. After everything Queenie put you through, you deserve a better life. You are not a prisoner, Princess. That door is not locked. You're free to roam the grounds as you see fit."

"If I can't go back to my home, I'm a fucking prisoner. Let me enlighten your ass. I had a better life that Hercules had given me. Whatever you're trying to give me, I don't want it. You snatched me away from my son, your grandchild. How can you possibly think that I would ever be willing to be happy to be held against my will? You and Hector betrayed the only man that has ever loved me for me. For that, I'll never forgive you. I'll die honoring that nigga because he basically died trying to give me a better life. Had he never met me he would be alive, so I'm not trying to hear shit, not mention the fact that you played Queenie. Losing you hurt her entire existence. She stood up for you and lost all respect because you were considered a rat. You threw her to the wolves and went on about your life. Did you know she's been strung out on heroin damn near all my life? She was finally getting clean and able to be a mother to me, but you fucked that up. I'm almost positive she has left rehab and started back using not knowing where I am. Shame on you; you should be tired of hurting us."

I was waiting for him to respond, but instead, he walked out of the room. The truth hurts, and I pray it eats his coward ass alive.

AFTER BEING in the room for so long, I decided to finally come out. Sophia was in desperate need of fresh air. I believe the room that we had been in was making her sick. She's become so pale, and I was afraid. At the same time, that might work in my favor. If she became sick enough, they might have to get her to a hospital. That would help me be able to at least alert someone to get me a message back to the states.

As I passed a mirror in the hallway, I cringed looking at my appearance. I had lost so much weight that I looked like a damn skeleton. I was regretting going on a hunger strike. My hair was all over my head and matted. Another month like this I was sure to be looking like Whitney Houston on crack.

As soon as I walked down the stairs, the first person I saw was Hector. This nigga disgusted me. I had to swallow to keep from vomiting. He literally made me sick to my damn stomach.

"I'm so happy you decided to come out of the room, Princess," Benito said.

"Sophia isn't feeling so good. I just wanted to take her out back and let her run around to get fresh air."

"I'm going to call a doctor to come and look at her." Hector stared at me the entire time that I walked past them. I hated his ass with a passion.

"What's good, Princess? You not speaking to a nigga today." He tried grabbing my arm, but my reflexes slapped the fuck out of him.

"Don't say shit to me, you Judas! You're nothing but a snake ass nigga, and I don't fuck with snakes. Get your fat ass away from me."

"Hector! Don't you ever put your hands on my daughter again."

Benito had pulled a big ass sword from the wall and held it to his neck. Hector's eyes were wide as saucers. I could tell he felt stupid as fuck. Here it is he crossed his best friend, and now he is getting treated like a bitch nigga. I smirked at his ass and walked out of the patio door. Looking around, I noticed armed men everywhere. I couldn't get out if I wanted to.

"Doesn't the air feel good, Sophia?" I kissed her on the cheek as she clapped her hands. The smile on her face warmed my heart. This was probably the first time I had ever seen her smile. Benito's estate was absolutely beautiful. Under normal circumstances, I would have loved for him to bring me here so that I could get to know him. He did this shit all wrong, and now I despise him.

"She is so beautiful?" Passion said as she came and sat next to me on the patio.

"Thank you," I responded dry as hell.

"I was thinking maybe you and I could get to know each other better."

"I was thinking the fuck not! Listen, Passion. I don't know if you understand what's going on, but I've been kidnapped. Hector and our father brought me here against my will. They killed the love of my life and made my newborn a fucking orphan. So, excuse me if I'm not in the mood to play sister to a person I don't need to know."

I hated to be mean to her, but she was getting on my nerves walking around playing slow. Like, bitch you know they kidnapped me.

"Hercules is not dead."

"Huh?" I had to make sure I had heard her correctly.

"At first I didn't know that you were kidnapped. I actually didn't know that I had a sister until you showed up here all of a sudden. It wasn't until I heard him and my mother arguing about you. That's when I learned what went down. Earlier today Hector came back from Chicago and informed our father that Hercules is alive but in a coma. Don't worry about your son. Your mother is now living in the house taking care of him and helping out with Hercules care. I've been lied to all of my life just like you by that man. We need to come together because we both need to get something out of this. I've lived in Medellin all of my life, and after this shit, I want out. If you take me back to the states with you, I'll help you escape."

I stared at her for a long time before even responding. This had to be some type of joke. For all I know she's working for them.

"Why do you want to help me? Are you really ready to leave this life of luxury to go to Chicago? Not to mention you don't know me from a can of paint. Why would you risk your life for mine?"

"This life is a lie and a big ass façade! My father is a liar and a criminal. My mother is a weak woman for my father, and I can't take it anymore. For her to know he kidnapped you and not say anything to him about it is beyond me. She's more concerned about him bringing his side bitch's baby into her house."

"It's so crazy that my mom is back in Chicago under the impression that he's serving a life sentence, and he was all for her before getting locked up. She has no idea he had a whole life here."

"That's so crazy because he's been around my whole life, and I've never even heard of him being in prison."

I just shook my head listening. This man fucked Queenie over in the worse way. Although I'm the one that's being held against my will, I feel extremely bad for her.

"No. The crazy part is that my mother has always known about my father's relationship with Queenie and your existence. She has never spoken on it until you arrived here. I'm telling you their argument was so loud that I'm surprised you didn't hear it."

"How do you plan on getting us out of here?" I needed to know what the hell her plan was at this point. She was in her feelings, and I needed to play on that shit.

For a minute, I stared at her and realized we were damn near identical. Although I didn't care to get to know her, I had to admit it was pretty cool having a sister. Growing up as the only child was boring as fuck.

"By seducing Hector?"

"Say what now?"

"You see what our father doesn't know is that Hector has a thing for me. I always catch him looking at my ass. Once I caught him jacking off as I undressed. You see he is the key to us getting to Chicago. That fat motherfucker will sell his soul for some pussy. Once I put a bullet in his head we out of here."

"I don't think that shit will work. Benito is not a fool, nor is Hector."

"Yes, it will. Hector is a dumb ass. He'll never see it coming. I just need you to act like you're coming around with the idea of being here. That's the only way our father will put his guards down in the event that the Hector idea doesn't work. You see you are Benito's biggest regret. He hates how things turned out for you, so he's willing to do anything to win you over. You see at first he was on some devious shit when he kidnapped you. Now he sees how much he has hurt you, and he wants to make amends. Once he lets his guards down, we're gone. "

"I appreciate you trying to help me, but I feel like the reason you gave me is not valid enough to go against the people who raised you. You don't even know me. I don't mean to say it that way, but I just feel like there is something more you're not telling me."

Her plan sounded like we could pull off, but this shit was more personal than she was letting on. Yes, she wanted to help me, but I feel like this was more for her benefit. I stared at her as she twiddled her thumbs a little bit and contemplated what she was about to say.

"I'm being honest with you. After hearing the shit they were arguing about, I knew that I could no longer stay here. I've been in Medellin all my life and living under their rule. I'm about to be twenty-three, and I've never seen the world. Plus, if he can do this to you, who's to say he won't do something fucked up to me. I want out of this country and away from them. Just give me a chance. I mean, after all, we are sisters."

"Okay, but don't even think about crossing me because to get back home to my son I'll kill you and everybody in this house if I have to." I meant every word I said.

Looking around the premises, they were heavily guarded, so there was no way I would ever be able just to walk or run off. I had to go along with Passion's plan in order to get home. I was relieved to find out Herc was alive, but him being in a coma was still too much. When he woke up, I needed to be the first person that he saw. This plan better had work. I needed to get back to my nigga and most importantly my son.

TWO

QUEENIE

In light of recent events, one would think that I would have run to the dope spot. That's the last place I was thinking about. The only thing on my mind was finding my baby and my granddaughter. We were finally starting to mend our relationship, and she vanishes. It's been two months, and I'm about ready to lose my mind. One thing that I know for a fact about Princess is that she would not leave Herc or her son willingly. At first, we all thought she had left until her car was found ditched in the parking lot of an abandoned warehouse. Somebody snatched her and my granddaughter. For the first time, I wish Lucifer was alive and that he had her. He was the only one who had a motive to take them.

Besides trying to keep my mind right, it was a job taking care of my grandson.

The minute I found out that she was kidnapped, and Herc had been shot up, I checked myself out of the hospital. Since that day Miami, Marisol, and I have been holding shit down. Between taking care of Baby Herc, I've been trafficking for Marisol in an effort to keep the money flowing. Miami had a lot on her plate. Herc was still in a coma, and she had him moved in the house with medical staff

PRINCESS AND THE PLUG 2   23

taking care of him around the clock. She was also pregnant by Diego and taking care of Brittani and Ziyon. I moved in to help out because she couldn't do this shit on her own. Marisol had moved in to help out too. The entire house was feeling the pain of Princess being gone and Herc being in a coma.

Bonnie and Clyde had got sick at one point because they were refusing to eat. We ended up having to move them inside of the room Herc was being held in an effort to get them to eat. Now they're okay and back to getting all types of bullshit. I'm about ready to ship their asses to Brookfield Zoo. Those monkeys are not normal. You can't even leave your liquor around them because they drink it.

I had just come from a run, and I was laid in bed next to my grandson. He was getting so fat. Princess was going to have a fit when she saw him. She kept saying she didn't want her baby to be all chunky. His ass is greedy, and if he keeps this shit up, he'll be a big ass kid.

"Ms. Queenie, I can take him a little while so you can rest."

"Are you sure Delilah? I know you're exhausted." Delilah had been a godsend as well. She was the rock we all needed when we got tired.

"I'm sure. It's both of our naptime anyway. We watch *General Hospital* every day, and then we nap. That's me and his thing." She picked him up from the bed and walked out of the room.

I found myself quickly dozing off with nothing but thoughts of my daughter and granddaughter. *Where the fuck can they be?*

"HERCULES, it's time for you to wake your ass up! Princess is still missing and needs your help," I spoke to him as I rubbed his hands with lotion.

He gripped my hand as usual, which was a good sign. Every time anyone said Princess' name he tries moving around. We had to strap his hands down before he knocked a tube or something a loose.

"How is he doing?" Hector asked as he entered the room.

"He's about the same. How did the run go to Medellin?"

I had to ask because he had been staying longer in Medellin each run and that was out of the ordinary. He would always come back days later than we expected him and that threw the rest of our runs off schedule. We had our shit down pact, and Hector was throwing us off.

"It went well. It's just that it's hard for me to get back through customs when I get over there."

Hearing him say customs kind of threw me off. We use private planes to do all of our transports. I know damn well there are no customs agents in the damn sky pulling planes over. Lately, Hector has been giving me some mixed signals. He's so lackluster about this entire situation. He and Hercules are like the best of friends, not to mention he's like security for him, and his behavior is off. I haven't spoken on it to anyone because they will think I'm crazy. People tend not to believe the local crack head. Although I don't use anymore, I'm still being watched like a hawk. Everything I do is questionable in my counterpart's eyes.

"Oh okay. Well, at least you don't have to go back until next month."

"Actually, it's some things Herc had me checking out before all of this happened, so I'll be headed back this weekend. I'm just trying to make sure shit doesn't fall through with Herc being out of commission."

"That's what up. Have you found any leads on who took Princess?" Herc gripped my hand tight again hearing Princess' name.

"Not yet and the streets aren't talking at all. I'm about to head back out and see if our people got anything." Hector spoke to me the entire time with his head in his phone. He could care less about my daughter, and it showed.

Before I got hooked on that shit, I was in the streets. Benito taught me how to read people, and this motherfucker in front of me was not to be trusted. Without a word, he left the room. One of the things that stood out to me was the fact that he never approached Herc's bed anytime he came in the room and I was in there. Real friends hold vigils at their friend's bedside. I smell a rat, and it is starting to really stink.

The sound of the doorbell ringing made me rush to the door. Looking at the screen on the wall before opening it, I realized it was the neighbor that lived up the road.

"Hi! Can I help you?"

"Yes, I'm looking for Mr. Hernandez."

"I'm sorry. He's not home. Maybe I can help you. Please step inside, ma'am."

I stepped to the side and allowed her in. We were keeping Hercules condition under wraps. As far as the streets knew he was dead. Her asking about him lets me know she doesn't even know about him being hit up.

"Is that a monkey?" she stuttered.

"Yes, she's harmless but bad as fuck. Please come and have a seat."

Bonnie was sitting on the couch in my damn purse. She had my damn compact mirror putting on lipstick. The lady was scared as hell, and I was trying my best to hold in my laugh. Bonnie pissed me off making duck lips at the woman showing off her lipstick. She looked a hot damn mess with that shit everywhere.

"I'm Nomi. I have been battling myself with this because I've been afraid, but I needed to show him the picture of this man I saw taking pictures of his girlfriend Princess at the supermarket. I know that she's missing, and it's been weighing heavy on me since I heard about it.

"What picture?"

"This one."

My heart palpitated looking at Victor Garza. He and Benito were best friends back in the day. You didn't see one without the other. If he was following my baby around, then her father was around lurking somewhere.

"Thank you. I'm Princess' mother, Queenie. This is really helpful."

"My husband would kill me if he knew I showed you this. He told me to stay out of it, but I can't any longer. He met up with Mr. Hernandez' bodyguard outside when I was in the supermarket. I don't know his name, but it's the one that's on the hefty side. The whole scene was off because he was the one escorting her to the supermarket. They exchanged a big envelope too. Please make sure you tell Mr. Hernandez, but don't mention my name. He and my husband play golf sometimes, and he hates when I overstep my boundaries with his business associates if you get my drift." She winked her eye and hurriedly rushed out of the door. I was beside myself because I knew this nigga Hector was an opp ass nigga as the young people call them these days.

The sound of my grandson crying over the baby monitor I had on my pocket made me rush up the stairs to the nursery. As I rocked him back and forth to calm him down, I found myself thinking about how to proceed. I could either tell Marisol, Diego, and Miami, or I could handle shit myself. I may have become weak in regards to the drugs, but I was no punk ass bitch when it came down to toting my pistol.

Things started to make sense the more I thought about shit. Many years ago before Benito was charged with anything, Victor fled to Medellin. It was all making sense now. Thank God for nosey ass neighbors because I would never have put two and two together.

"Don't you worry, Baby Herc. Grandma is going to bring your momma and sister home." He was just staring and smiling at me like he really knew what I was talking about.

Grandma was going to make shit right with his momma even if it meant losing my life in the process. I would gladly put my life on the line if it meant saving Princess and giving her a chance to enjoy her new life with Hercules. Lord, knows I ruined her early life already. She deserves a happily ever after.

THREE

MIAMI

Hercules needed to wake his ass the fuck up. Running this damn organization was getting the best of me. Being pregnant and trying to hold shit down was becoming too much on me. I don't know where I would be without Diego, Marisol, Queenie, and Hector. We've been holding it down, and I know that Herc would be so proud. Hector has been throwing the schedule off from time to time, but other than that, shit has been cool.

Hercules being in a coma and Princess being missing was weighing heavy on all of us, especially the kids. Brittani and Ziyon were having a really hard time. They're so used to spending time with their dad and him not being awake is hurting them. Hell, I'm hurting because I need him to get up and find Princess.

That baby needs his mother and father. Right now, neither of them are available, and it's heartbreaking. I'm so proud of Queenie for stepping up. I truly believe she's done with them damn drugs this time. That bitch has stepped up and jumped back into the drug game full speed ahead. She has been bringing in bags too. Whenever Herc wakes up, he's not going to be able to believe this shit.

"YOUR ASS NEEDS TO REST. All of this running around can't be good for the baby." Diego was lying across the bed watching me as I got dressed.

I needed to meet up with Marisol so that we could handle this last run for the month. We had to get the drugs from the girls and get them back on the plane to their original cities. As much as I wanted to sit down and put my feet up, I couldn't. Money still has to be made, and Herc would kick our asses if we let the family lose money.

"This is the last run, baby. I promise I'll rest after this."

I had to go over and start kissing and loving on him. Diego was so damn needy. He needed my attention every second of the day, and I loved that shit. Diego wanted to lay up in this pussy all day if he could. I have no problem with letting him either.

"Don't try that shit with me. You're pregnant with my seed now, and I'm not risking you losing it behind this shit. I'll take up the extra shit to keep the money flow. I know that you feel like you owe Herc for how good he has been to you and Brittani. However, you're my wife now, and we're building our family. Trust me. Herc will understand. Now bend over, I need to feel you."

Diego was always so straight forward with the way he was feeling. He let it be known, and it didn't matter what it was. That's why I love him so much. He accepts my bond with Herc but always makes sure to remind me that I belong to him. Without hesitation, I bent my ass over and let my nigga go in for the kill. He still has my pussy sore as no matter how much we fuck. Diego's got the type of dick that's long and thick as hell. That's one of the reasons why I'm so damn sprung on him. His dick game was official, and he had my ass addicted and dick silly for real. I can't believe I'm getting ready to have his baby. Never in my wildest dreams did I think I would have the type of love that I have with Diego. Herc is that once upon a time love that you never get again. Despite our downfalls, he was special, and I always felt like no man could ever replace him, but Diego has shown up and shown the fuck out. There is nothing like a man that comes into your life and gives you purpose, not to mention the will to give your heart again. I've never loved anyone this way since Herc. This nigga got my heart. I just pray he doesn't make me regret this shit.

"PUT THAT SHIT OUT, MARISOL!" This bitch had been smoking back to back. I just knew my baby was inhaling all the damn second smoke.

"Look, your pregnant ass should have stayed home with all of this complaining. You know if I don't have my weed, I can't think, bitch!"

"You can't do shit without that damn weed. Let's hurry up so that I can get back to the house. I miss Diego."

"Bitch! You just left him and all that damn screaming your ass was doing you should want to give your pussy a break."

"Oh my God! You heard me?"

"We all heard you. Hell, I'm surprised Herc didn't wake up and hear your ass." I covered my face in embarrassment hearing that shit.

"That be Diego fucking me like he a maniac. He be having my ass crawling the walls and shit.

"That's what up. I'm so happy for you."

"He makes me so happy, Marisol. I'm so happy that I got the courage to come clean and let Herc know about us. His reaction was surprising. I just knew that he was going to go crazy, but he embraced us. I think it had a lot to do with Princess. He was ready to be happy again, and he knew I deserved happiness too. I just wish he'd wake up so that we can find her."

I choked up speaking on Princess. Her being missing is weighing thin on my spirit. The house is so dim without her. I can truly say she brightened up the place cause that bitch Bleu made it sinister as hell. Just thinking about how this crazy bitch killed Mrs. Hernandez has me shook, not to mention killed her own damn momma. About a month after Princess kidnapping and Herc's shooting we found out her mother was killed in a hotel room. Her fingerprints were all over the statue. The police had an APB out on her crazy ass. Little did they know that bitch was sleeping with the fishes. I'm happy Herc murked her ass. We can all sleep a little better knowing she is not alive to hurt people.

"I just keep thinking where she could be and why she would leave and not tell anyone. While she was out getting her baby, Herc was also out trying to get her. I just wish they would have told each other their plans. None of this shit would be happening the way it is. Wherever she is, I pray that she and her daughter are okay. Princess has to be found before Herc wakes up. If he wakes up and she's still gone, it's going to be a massacre, and no one is safe."

Just sitting in the passenger seat, I didn't know what else to say about it. I wish I could wake up and this shit would all be a dream. About twenty minutes later, we were pulling up to the Hyatt Regency Hotel. I immediately got pissed looking at the mules standing outside and not in the room.

"Why the fuck aren't you in the room?" Marisol jumped out and asked through gritted teeth.

"There were no rooms in our names."

"Hector was supposed to book the rooms. Let me call his ass." Pulling out my phone, I called his ass repeatedly, and he never answered.

"I'll book the room now. Y'all good?" Marisol asked concerned. The shit had me shook because the drugs had been in them longer than they should have been. Hector was supposed to meet them here and start removing the balloons so that when we made it, we could pay them and be on our way. Looking at the mules they both looked fine, but the last thing we needed was for one of the balloons to burst inside of them.

Walking inside of the hotel, we hurriedly booked a room and got the balloons removed. This motherfucker Hector was still not answering. I called Diego, and he was livid. Lately, Hector has been doing shit his way, and that was not cool. If Hercules weren't in a damn coma, he wouldn't dare be doing this shit. As we checked inside of the room, Marisol and I both waited while the girls passed the balloons.

"This shit is not good. What the fuck is going on with Hector? The nigga has been fucking up lately. I'm surprised because he's usually by the book no matter what. I know damn well he ain't trying to be on no other shit because Herc is in a coma."

I hated to say the shit but the way Hector moving right now is not sitting right with me. No matter what, we work as a team. Because we have kept shit the same way for years, we've all managed to stay out of prison and steps ahead of the laws. This nigga will not have me sitting in prison behind his dumb shit.

"This nigga got me so heated. I need a damn blunt to calm my nerves!"

I just shook my head at Marisol. She just smoked three damn blunts. There ain't no way she needs another one. Then again, I need a damn blunt at this point in time.

After getting all of the balloons and paying the girls, we headed back to the house. Walking inside of the house, I almost passed the fuck out looking at Herc sitting on the couch. Bonnie and Clyde were all over him. He looked pale as ever, and it was scary.

"I'm so glad y'all made it back. Help me get him back in the bed. I was napping with the baby and heard a crash. I was running around like a crazy person and found his ass out here on the floor. I sent the kids to the guesthouse with Delilah. They don't need to see him like this.

"We can't lift his big ass. Where is Hector or Diego at?"

"I've tried calling Hector, but he's not answering. Diego went out to check the traps. Let just make him comfortable right here on the couch until the doctor and nurse arrive. I've already called them."

"Where Princess at?" he slurred.

We all just stood quiet and not answering the question. He was staring at me intensely trying to read me, but I made sure not to make eye contact. Instead, I hopped in and started trying to make him as comfortable as possible on the couch. He gripped his chest, and I knew he was in a lot of pain. Marisol, Queenie, and I got Herc situated, and he was trying his best to fight with us.

"Just calm down, Hercules." I had to hold in my tears because he looked like he was emotional and starting to remember.

Before we could say anything, the medical staff we had hired arrived and started taking his vitals. We stood around looking lost. I know that we were all relieved that he woke up from the coma. At the same time, Princess was still missing, and the beast within was about to wreak havoc on the streets of Chicago.

FOUR

HERCULES

I didn't want to be sitting in a fucking hospital bed. A nigga needed to be out trying to find Princess. For the first time in my life, a nigga was feeling helpless. Not Hercules Hernandez, I'm the nigga that gets the motherfucking job done. This shit with Princess being missing and me being hit up got me angry as fuck. Niggas think shit sweet or think I'm getting soft out here in these streets. That shit the bitch Bleu pulled wasn't cool at all. I'm almost positive the streets were aware of that shit and think a nigga is soft behind it. I'm the same nigga I've always been, and I'll still kill anything moving if it's a threat. Right now, motherfuckers definitely have a death wish. It's one thing to try and kill me, but to touch what the fuck belongs to me is totally different. Princess had birthed my seed and gave me one of the most precious things a woman could give a man. That off top made her mine. Niggas didn't know they had fucked with the wrong one.

I blamed myself for all of this shit. She was supposed to have a better life with me, not get into more shit. I was supposed to be her sanctuary. Instead, she was poisoned and kidnapped. I know she's not dead because I don't feel the shit in my heart. She's somewhere being held to spite me. It doesn't take a rocket scientist to link my shooting and her kidnapping. Both incidents happened the same night within hours of each other.

The police had been trying their best to get me to come in for questioning, but I wasn't feeling that shit. For all I knew, they were behind that shit, and I don't trust a soul. That added with the fact that I had no idea who had made an attempt on my life. I wish like hell I had because the motherfuckers would definitely be floating in the river some fucking where.

I had been out of the coma for a week, and the gunshot I suffered to my chest was the hardest to recover from. A nigga got out of breath walking to the bathroom, but I needed to get out and find both Princess and the person who was behind trying to kill me. Besides dealing with that, the numbers were off tremendously, and it was a cause for concern. The whole crew had been walking on eggshells around me, but today I needed them to explain what the fuck was going on.

MIAMI, Diego, Queenie, Marisol, Hector, Jigg, and I were all sitting around the family room.

"It's damn near one million dollars missing, and somebody needs to fucking explain." I winced in pain raising my voice. Miami instantly tried to jump up and rush over to my end of the table. I put my hand up gesturing for her to stop. Miami was too overprotective. I loved that she cared for me the way she does. At the same time, she's with Diego now, and I can't allow her to be disrespectful. Even though she doesn't intentionally mean to be disrespectful, as a man, its certain shit I will not allow my woman to do in regards to another nigga.

"I went over the numbers, and things panned all out. I'm not sure how a million dollars is missing," Hector proudly responded like it was cool for him to speak on like I'm lying or some shit.

"A million dollars is missing, and I need to know where the fuck it is. That type of bread does not just disappear!" This nigga was too fucking nonchalant for my liking.

"Maybe Hector left it in Medellin!" Queenie said as she jumped up aiming a gun at him.

"You crazy crackhead ass bitch! What the fuck are you trying to say?"

"Put the gun down, Queenie!" Miami pleaded.

I was sitting in shock behind the display in front of me. I didn't know Queenie fucked with me so heavy that she would go hard about my missing money. Then again, Marisol and Miami have spoken highly of how she has held shit down in my absence.

"What do you mean by that, Queenie?" I inquired while searching Hector's face. He was like a deer in headlights and surprised just like we were.

"Are you going to stand here and act like I'm crazy or are you going to come clean?"

"Man, Hercules, I don't even know why you're letting this crackhead ass bitch in your crib. For all we know, she's stealing shit to go get high with!"

"If you know something Queenie, you need to spill that shit!" Diego yelled.

"Hector helped Benito kidnap Princess. My daughter and granddaughter are over in Medellin. Look, here he is with Victor Garza. This is Benito's best friend. If Hector is having any dealings with Victor, he has to have dealings with Benito!"

I balled up my fist and clenched my jaws looking at the picture of Hector with the nigga Victor whom I knew as Pablo, Juan's right hand man. Without hesitation, I shot his ass in both of his legs.

"I'm sorry, Herc! Juan and his crew threatened to kill my whole family!" The nigga was rolling around on the floor like the bitch he was with his big ass.

"So you sacrifice my motherfucking family! It's blood in and blood out with the Hernandez Cartel. I'm willing to die behind this shit. That's why I have it branded on me. You vowed the same, but nigga you ain't built for this shit! Instead of going against the grain, you should have paid with your life!

I knew you were moving funny style lately. There's always a Judas at every fucking table, and that's why you have to watch who you eat with! Since I now know you were behind Princess' disappearance, keep it real and tell me that you tried to take me out!"

"I'm sorry, Herc! I had no choice."

Hearing him cry and admit the shit fucked me up because he was my right hand and one of the people on the team that I trusted the most. Shit like this hurts a nigga like me because I took that nigga from the gutter and introduced him and his family to the good fucking life, and this is the thanks I get.

"We murking this nigga or what?" Jigg interjected as he stood over him with his gun pressed to his forehead.

"In due time. Take him to the slaughterhouse and beat this nigga ass until he tells you exactly where that nigga is keeping Princess and where the fuck my bread is at!

On command, Jigg and Diego started dragging that nigga out.

"Please Herc, don't do this! I'll tell you whatever you need to know."

"Miami, get in contact with the pilot and let him know will be flying to Medellin first thing in the morning. Marisol, you stay here and keep shit in order. Queenie, you're going with us."

I didn't give any of them a chance to respond. I really didn't want any objections to my order. The only thing I was focused on was getting Princess and Sophia back home.

FOR THE FIRST time since I woke up, I was spending time with my kids. I had been avoiding them simply because I couldn't bear to look at them in my current state. The pain I was in didn't even allow me to hold my son, and I had already missed out on so much being in a coma. It was hard for me to look at him because it was a reminder that his mother was missing. I was livid that she was in the care of a nigga that portrayed himself to be an associate. At the same time, she doesn't know that nigga from a can of paint. How could he ever think taking her would be a good idea? He's a fucking stranger. At the same time, I can't wait to confront the nigga about this shit. If he wanted to know his daughter, he could have just reached out. Then again, this the same motherfucker that was supposedly in jail for life.

Looking over at Ziyon and Brittani, they were both knocked out in bed with me. They cried until I just gave in. All I could think about was leaving them. Even in the afterlife, I would have been mad at myself for letting this nigga catch me slipping.

"What's up, son? You getting fat on your daddy?"

Baby Herc was huge for only three months. Queenie had to be feeding him more than milk. Peeking over into his crib, I tugged at his hand. He immediately gripped it, and I knew he was strong. I couldn't wait to get Princess back home where she belongs. I had so many plans for us before all of this shit happened, and I have every intention on following through with it. I wasn't a praying nigga, but before I fell asleep with my children, I prayed over my household.

THE NEXT MORNING I woke up and ready to get to Medellin so that I could fuck some shit up. I could tell Queenie was nervous. This shit was deep for her. The father of her child who she thought had a life sentence had been living a double life. I'm almost positive that shit was fucking with her in the worst way.

"Are you okay, Hercules? Do you need some pain medicine?" Queenie asked concerned.

"Nah! I'm good. This Kush got me feeling good and relaxed. By the time the plane takes off, I'll be able to rest. The question is how are you doing."

"I'll be okay as soon as I have my daughter and granddaughter in my possession. As much as I'm hurt and feel like I don't even want an explanation from him, I've gotten my life back on track, and the only thing that matters is getting the relationship I want with my daughter. His absence destroyed us, and I refuse to allow his presence to destroy us further. The only thing that's keeping me calm is that I know he would never hurt her."

"I'm proud of you, Queenie. I can't wait to tell Princess about how much progress you made and how you stood up when we needed you the most. Trust me that shit won't go unpaid. Now let's get through this long ass plane ride so that we get our girls back."

Before taking off, I received an unexpected call from an unlikely source. I should have shared the information with Queenie, but she might try and do too much with getting Princess back. I decided to sit on the shit until after I pulled the shit off. The call I received made this shit much easier because I didn't have time to be running all over Medellin trying to find this bitch ass nigga Benito.

FIVE

PASSION

I should have listened to Princess when she said seducing Hector wouldn't be easy. That nigga wasn't biting period. I actually realized he was more interested in Princess. It was weird as hell watching how he watched her. The shit was creepy as hell. It made me wonder just how much he probably watched her back home in Chicago when Hercules wasn't around.

Speaking of Hercules, I couldn't wait to get Princess back home to him. The way she talks about him is something out of a fairytale. I can only hope to find someone like that. My father was feared out here in Medellin, so no man would ever even attempt to come at me. My grown ass was still a virgin. That's the part I didn't tell Princess. That's another reason I wanted to leave this God forsaken place. It's the only way I'll be able to live a normal life. I want to find love and have children just like Princess.

Through the many conversations that Princess and I have had about her life, it makes me want to try to convince my father to let her go home. He had been away on business the past week, but we had heavy security presence on the estate, so we couldn't leave if we tried to. Since he was gone, I decided to try to talk some sense into my mother. She was walking around with blinders on. At first, she was being a bitch to Princess, and now she was walking around being nice. I'm almost positive that's because my father dug in her ass for the way she had been treating Princess. My mother is like Cruella Deville, so I know she has something up her sleeve. I just needed to find out what the hell it was.

I rolled my eyes as I walked inside of her parlor. She was sipping on what I'm sure was her tenth martini of the day.

"Can I talk to you for a minute?"

"Is it important? You know I don't like to be bothered when I'm having my martini?"

"Well, that means you never want to be bothered because you drink all day."

All of my life I've dealt with being pushed to the side or put off on the help. It's sad when a mother is so self-centered that she instructs the maid to teach you about your period. Growing up, I thought the world of my mother because everyone else around her did. My mother was beautiful like the Latin actress Sofia Vergara with the body to match. The older I got, I realized she was beautiful on the outside but ugly as fuck on the inside. At this point, I don't even think I love her. I just tolerate her because she's the woman that gave me life.

"I don't have time, Passion."

"Well since you don't have time let me make this quick. I think that you need to let Princess and her daughter go home. You need to do the right thing instead of walking here staying drunk.

"Princess and her daughter aren't my problem. Tell your father that when he comes back. I could care less."

"You are a pitiful excuse for a woman. I can see you being in your feelings about her being here knowing that daddy cheated on you. However, she's being held against her will. I've always known that you were self-centered, but I never took you to be a heartless bitch."

The fact that she was stirring her martini and laughing like something was funny was beyond me.

"You sitting here acting like you care so much is comical. Why haven't you freed her? I mean you're walking around all up in her ass. I'm surprised you don't know what her shit smell like. I've been watching you walking around here acting like she really somebody. She's a whore and the daughter of a crack head. There ain't a damn thing special about her ass. As far as I'm concerned, she can be stuck here the rest of her life because I'm leaving my damn self. It won't be long before they come to raid this place or kill every motherfucker in here. Your daddy fucked with the Hernandez Cartel, and with Hercules not being dead, I can assure you it's only a matter of time before they come. I'm not the smartest person, but I wouldn't be surprised if he has already ditched our asses. I've been disconnected from you since birth, and now that you're grown, I suggest you go out in the world and find who you are. I got lost in your father, and I'm done. I suggest you get out while you can. Trust me. I won't stop you."

For a minute, I sat observing her, and I had no idea who she was. The feisty Estelita I know would not be sitting so content. I guess this is her being content and accepting that my father doesn't care about anybody but himself. Instead of saying anything to her, I headed towards my room and started grabbing as much of the money that I could. My parents didn't believe in banks, so money was hidden throughout the estate. It's crazy how one day you can be naïve to everything around you, then the next you're eyes are wide open to the bullshit. After grabbing as much money as I could, I placed it in duffle bags and started dragging the bags down the stairs.

"What are you doing?" Princess asked, standing at the top of the stairs.

Before I could answer, there was a loud bang that came from outside followed by gunfire. Peeking out the window, I watched as Jeeps and army tanks bussed through the front gates. I was stuck watching the guards basically get ran over and shot down. It literally looked like a battle on the front lawn.

Watching men jump from the jeeps with machetes and assault

rifles made me haul ass upstairs. My mother was in the hallway on her knees praying with her rosary beads clenched tight. I ran right past her in search of Princess and Sophia. The sound of the door crashing in paralyzed me because fear took over. It sounded like an army of men running up the stairs. That's when I heard more gunfire erupting. This time it was so close that the bullets were bouncing off of the wooden banister along the spiral staircase. It was literally like a scene from *Scarface*.

I hit the deck quick crawling into the room where Princess was being held. I found them underneath the bed. Princess was covering Sophia's mouth to mask her crying. I climbed right underneath the bed with them. Without hesitation, both Princess and I gripped each other's hand. Although gunfire was still erupting around us, I could still hear my mother praying loudly. Then all of a sudden, the praying stopped with a gunshot. That made my heart speed up because I knew they had murdered her.

"Princess!" The sound of a male voice calling her made me stop in my tracks.

"Princess! It's me, baby! Where you at?"

Without hesitation, Princess let my hand go and quickly grabbed Sophia. I was scared to move, but I slid from underneath the bed as well.

"Herc! You came and got us!" Princess jumped over my momma's body and basically collapsed in Herc's arms.

"What you thought I wasn't coming or something? Who the fuck is that?" He aimed a big ass gun at me, and I quickly jumped back with my hands up.

"Nooo! That's my sister. She's been trying to help me. We have to take her with us." I could look at him and tell he wasn't feeling that shit, but he quickly gave in.

"If I even think you're a snake like your people, I'll put a bullet in your head just like I did this bitch." He pointed the gun down at my mother, and I quickly looked away. She no longer had a head.

I was hurt to a certain extent because she was still my mother, but then again, how could I ever hurt over a woman who just minutes earlier told me she was disconnected from me.

"I'm nothing like them. I just want a new life and to build a relationship with my sister, niece, and nephew."

Princess reached her hand out to me, and I stepped over my mother's body to grab her hand. I didn't even look back at her. It would be like looking back on the past, and I was done with it.

"Let's get the fuck out of here!"

He grabbed Sophia from Princess, and they basically ran out of the house with me running right with them. I made sure to grab the duffle bags of money I previously had. When we made it outside, all of the men were basically standing around with big ass guns in silence. A beautiful woman hopped from one of the Jeeps and ran towards Princess. That had to be her mom Queenie. Just looking at how they doted on Princess was everything. I could only wish to have it.

As we rode the plane to Chicago, I could tell Queenie was irritated by my presence, which was understandable. I had no idea what was to come for my new life in Chicago, but I was going to make the best of it. Thoughts of my father crossed my mind. I didn't know if he was alive or dead. I really didn't care at this point. Either way he was as dead to me as my mother really was.

SIX

PRINCESS

Since being back home, I've done nothing but immerse myself in being a mother. Having Sophia and Baby Herc was a job, and I was loving every minute of it, not to mention taking care of Ziyon. Because I wanted to be hands-on with the kids, I was refusing to allow Delilah to do a lot of things she would normally do. Plus, I just wanted to catch up on the time that I had missed out on. It had been two weeks since Herc rescued me and the dynamic in the house is weird. For some reason, I feel like he is avoiding me, but I know the events really fucked with him mentally.

I'm happy that my sister has adapted in such a short time. The money that she took before getting out of Medellin was enough for her to sit on her ass for a long time. I still had my condo, so I gave it to her to live in. It was obvious Herc wasn't going to allow me to go back, so there was no need for it to go to just sit and collect dust.

Herc suggested that Passion lives in the house with us, but I flat out refused. I don't know her like that, but I was appreciative for her looking out for Sophia and me in Medellin. As long as I'm in Hercules' life, no other woman will be moving in here.

"Get out of here, Bonnie! I told you no more lipstick today. I don't care about you pouting. Get off of my vanity right now!"

She tried her best to look sad. When she noticed that I wasn't giving in, she jumped out of the chair and ran out of the room. That monkey had some major attitude issues.

As I sat on the edge of the bed, I ran my hands through my wild hair. The moment it got stuck, I realized I really needed to go to the salon. Getting up to look into the floor length mirror, I realized I looked popped. No wonder Herc was avoiding my ass. It was early, and the kids were napping, so I decided to have Delilah keep an eye on them and have a spa day with my sister. We had yet to really spend some time together since we got here other than she would come over for dinner, and we would watch movies.

I knew Herc would be upset with me if I didn't get his approval before going. The last time I did some shit with his approval I ended up kidnapped in another fucking country.

Once I got dressed, I headed to his office. As I walked inside, I observed him on the phone in a heated conversation. He stared at me intensely, and I couldn't read him.

"Let me hit you back!" He slammed the phone down and flamed up a blunt all the while staring at me as if I had something on my face.

"Is everything okay?"

"Why you dressed up?"

"I'm getting ready to go out and have a spa day with Passion."

"No, you not. In case you forgot, Benito is still out there. I just went through hell and high water getting you back home. We're not taking any risks, and I don't trust anyone outside of our immediate circle. Now if you want, I'll call in a glam crew for you and Passion, but going out is negative."

"I'll be okay, Herc. While I'm there, I'll make sure to call you the entire time we're gone. My hair is a mess, my toes and nails are hideous, not to mention I need to get a Brazilian wax. Herc I really need to get some air."

I hated to sound like a whiny brat, but he was being so dramatic.

"I said no! End of fucking discussion, Princess!" He slammed his fists on the desk and quickly stood to his feet.

The last time he raised his voice was when he saw me for the first when he found out I was pregnant. My feelings were hurt then, and they're extremely hurt now. He had handled me with tender love and care since we made things official. Right now, the tears that had welled up in my eyes fell quickly. Before I could say anything, Delilah let her presence be known. Keeping my back to her, I wiped the tears from my face.

"Excuse me. Mr. Hernandez, you have a guest waiting for you downstairs."

"Take them into the conference room and get them some drinks. I'll be down shortly."

"Yes, Mr. Hernandez."

"I'm sorry for yelling." He lifted my chin and kissed me on the lips before heading out of his office.

My feelings were so hurt that I didn't even know what to do. As I headed back to our bedroom, I made sure to check on the kids. They were still asleep, so I took that as an opportunity to smoke me a fat ass blunt to calm my nerves. Lately, weed was the only thing keeping me sane.

As I sat on the bed and smoked, I watched the bedroom door open and in came none other than Clyde. The damn monkey could smell weed a mile away. He climbed up on the bed and cozied up next to me. I just shook my head and handed him the half a blunt. I laughed so hard because he was smoking like a damn champ. He and Bonnie really gave this house life because I don't know where we would be without them.

LATER IN THE evening as we sat down for dinner, I became irritated. Queenie, the kids, and I were sitting and eating the fried chicken and baked macaroni I had cooked. Hercules had left the house after his meeting and didn't say a word to me. At this point, it was obvious he was avoiding me. As I ate, I realized we hadn't sat down as a family since I came back home and I quickly became overwhelmed with it all.

"What's wrong, Princess?"

"Nothing I'm okay, Queenie."

"Don't lie to me."

"I don't know what's going on with Hercules. He's not the same man he was before I was kidnapped. It's like he's mean and disconnected from me."

"Can I be honest without you feeling like I'm overstepping my boundaries?"

"Be honest."

"That man loves you, Princess. He was beside himself when he came out of the coma and realized you had been kidnapped. Princess, you have to understand that man is not disconnected from you. Right now, he's on a rampage trying to find Benito, not to mention running a multi-million dollar empire that's in jeopardy due to the snakes in his camp. That man feels like he failed you. It's not that he doesn't want to be around you. It's just hard for him to look at you. Both of you have been through a lot. Instead of you feeling that way, just hold him down on the home front while he handles the street shit. Hercules is not Lucifer, and he's not a regular nigga of the block. He's the nigga that own the block and all the fucking houses on it. Stop that crying shit. You've cried enough. It's time to step up and be a part of the Hernandez Cartel. He needs a ride or die. Now when I say that I'm not talking about trafficking drugs and running shit, I'm talking about giving him the peace of mind that he needs on the home front to run his business. A man is nothing without a strong woman behind him. Every time you sit and cry, it looks weak. Hercules Hernandez doesn't have room for weak bitch shit. Now wipe your face. Let's eat dinner, put the kids to bed, and put that pussy on that nigga when he gets home."

"Ma! Not in front of the kids."

"I'm sorry. I got carried away spitting that knowledge."

"Thank you. I really needed that."

"No problem. I'm just happy to step up and help you. Thank you for allowing me to try to redeem myself as a parent and be in my grandbabies life. They just love they Nana Queenie! Ain't that right granny babies?"

"Yes!" they all said in unison.

I was so happy Ziyon was opening up and allowing us to love him. At first, he was quiet and shy, but now he has adapted to not having Bleu around. Regardless of what she did to me, I still feel really bad for him. No matter how she betrayed Herc, she was still his mother.

Staring across the table at Queenie, a part of me was happy that I found it in my heart to forgive. These past months I learned that forgiving her was for me and not for her. In order for me to move on and live a happy life, I needed to let that hurt go. I forgive Queenie for what she did to me, but I'll never forget it. I mean how could anyone forget that type of trauma. I find comfort in knowing that Lucifer is dead. He's no longer on this earth to turn out any woman or ruin their life. I know that human trafficking is still going on and will always be a problem. I'm grateful that I was one of the lucky ones that were rescued.

"How is Passion adapting?"

"She's actually doing better than I thought. The best thing Benito ever could have done was teach her English because she would have been fucked had she not known it. I could never allow her to live here, so I'm encouraging her independence. She had been staying over in the condo, and she has been coming over and spending time with us. I'm actually starting to love having a sister. Queenie, you're always rude to her, so I'm surprised that you're asking about her.

"It's not that I'm rude to her. I was just feeling her out. You don't know her, and I understand that she tried to help you when you needed her. After what this family has been through, I really don't trust a soul. Just be careful and don't be too trusting to tell her your personal business."

From the jump Queenie side eyed Passion. I know that when she looks at her, she feels betrayed, just like Estelita felt when she saw me in her home. Neither Passion nor I is responsible for this shit. Benito's coward ass is the one to blame for all of this shit. Now his ass is on the run from Herc. If he knows like I know, he better stay on the run because my nigga is out for blood.

"Trust me. She's not like that. Her ass wanted to be far out of there before you all ever showed up. She knew nothing about me and felt betrayed by her parents. She has suffered too behind his lies. Please try being nice to her."

"I'll try, but the first time she gives me an inkling that she's a snake I'm going to murder her ass. " The Queenie I was looking at was dying to kill somebody. Her recovery has old school Queenie back and in full effect.

For the rest of the night, we talked and put the kids to bed before she left. Since Hercules was still out, I decided to put on something sexy and wait for him to come home. I must have been exhausted because I woke up in the middle of the night to find Hercules asleep in the east wing of the house. I was mad, but I didn't let it deter me from climbing in bed and snuggling up under him. We still hadn't had sex, and I wanted to make love to him so bad. I had never been so sexually free with him out of fear that he would judge me. A bitch had to throw out them fears and go in for the kill. He was on his back asleep in nothing but his black and gold Versace boxers. The wounds on his chest from being shot looked painful even though he had gauze over them. Kissing him on his lips, I made a trail of kisses down his chest making sure to kiss his wounds. Slipping my hand into his boxers, I stroked his dick before placing the head in my mouth. Before I could even get into it good, he pushed me away and put his dick up.

"What's the problem, Herc?"

"There is no problem. I'm just not in the mood."

"What bitch you fucking that got you not in the mood?"

"The last thing on my mind is pussy, and a bitch is the furthest from my mind. Make that your last time questioning me."

I sat on the edge of the bed, and that's where I left his ass. He had me so fucked up! The nigga could stay not in the mood.

I woke up the next morning, and of course, he was gone. I took the kids to the guesthouse with Delilah, and I went and had my spa day. I'm not about to be sitting around here while he treats me as if he doesn't want to be bothered.

IT FELT SO good to have a fresh blow out. The Egyptians had my real hair so silky and pretty. I had been wearing weave for so long that I forgot I actually had beautiful ass hair. After getting my hair done, I headed to get me a full set and a pedicure. The way the nail tech massaged my feet had me bussing nuts in the damn massage chair. This spa day was definitely what I needed because it relieved some stress. At the same time, I was still in my feelings behind Herc's actions. Surprisingly, he hadn't called my phone, and I definitely didn't call his. After speaking with Queenie last night, I had it in my mind to be better, but his rejection angered me. I think I was more hurt than anything, and it made me react.

While getting my Brazilian wax, I noticed that the lady kept looking at the tattoo I had across the top of my pussy. Lucifer's name was still there big, bold, and absolutely embarrassing. Without hesitation, I headed to the nearest tattoo shop and got it covered with big beautiful roses. I shed a tear as I marveled at it in the mirror after the tattoo artist was done. I had never felt so free in my life. My heart was filled with so much joy. At that moment, no one owned me. My body was my temple, and it was mine. It ain't a nigga in this world that can touch me sexually unless I give them permission to, not that I want any nigga to touch me. The only man I want is Hercules Hernandez.

AFTER A LONG ASS DAY, I still wasn't ready to go home. I decided to go to Mz. Lady P's Place and have a drink. The Patrón Margarita I was sipping was good as hell. Just sitting there, all I could think of was the days I was locked up in that house with Lucifer and dreaming of one day having my freedom. This shit right here was the life I missed out on, and I deserved to live it.

"Can I buy you a drink?" I looked up to see a handsome guy standing over me. The shit kind of spooked me out because he appeared out of nowhere.

"No, thank you. I'm fine."

"Come on now. Let a nigga buy you drink, beautiful. It's obvious you don't have a man. A nigga like me would never let you out of the house unsupervised." He stroked my face, and before I could react, a gunshot went off.

The feeling of warm blood splattering on my face horrified me. His body dropped with a loud thud, and that's when I noticed Hercules. He sat on the barstool next to me like it was nothing. I was speechless looking at him place the smoking gun on the counter.

"Aye P! Let me get a double shot of Rémy." He loosened his tie and took a napkin from the bar. I jumped as he wiped the blood off of my face.

I couldn't believe everybody in the bar was acting as if there wasn't a man on the floor with his brains lying next to him. I mean everyone was still drinking and acting as if nothing had just happened.

"Here you go, boss." Mz. P handed him the drink, and he quickly knocked it back.

"Hercules I—"

He immediately put his hand up to stop me from talking.

"Go home! We'll talk about this later." I wanted to say something, but I grabbed my damn purse and got the hell out of dodge. Hercules had me so scared that I kept looking back to see if he was behind me.

The drive home seemed long as ever. Going inside of the house, I was met by Marisol, Miami, Queenie, and Passion. They were all looking at me with concerned eyes, but I didn't have time to talk to any of them, not to mention hear their mouth about me living. I rushed right past them and ran up the stairs.

"Don't run your ass up there! You had us scared!" Queenie yelled behind me, but I wasn't trying to hear it.

The house was so damn big it took forever for me to make it to my bedroom. I immediately stripped out of my clothes and started to scrub my skin. The smell of blood had me nauseous as fuck. So much for a fresh ass hair do I put my head under the water making sure to get every speck of blood off me that had splattered. My ass stayed in the shower and scrubbed until my skin was raw. After drying off, I walked into the bedroom and wanted to walk back into the shower. Herc was sitting on the edge of the bed smoking a blunt with the meanest mug on his face. I've started to see this mean ass nigga in a different light since he rescued me.

"Explain to me why you would go against my wishes and leave this house?"

"It wasn't that I was going against your wishes. I just needed a release. It's like ever since you rescued me, you've been distant. I've been walking around here trying to adapt to being a mother of three and dealing with being kidnapped, and you're walking around here as if I don't exist. In case you forgot, I've been hurt behind this shit too. Instead of paying me attention, you're walking around as if I did something to you. To make matters worse, I try to suck your dick and all of a sudden you're not in the mood. That shit really hurt my feelings, Hercules!"

"Let's get some shit straight! Lower your voice when you're talking to me. Stop yelling and stomping like a fucking brat that can't have her way. Since you want to speak on hurt feelings, let's discuss how the fuck you hurt mine.

While you were out doing shit behind my back to get Sophia, I was murking that nigga Lucifer. Imagine how the fuck I felt when I walked back in the crib to find you gone. I went in search of you immediately only to get hit up and wake up to find you had been kidnapped. None of that shit would have happened like that had you not gone behind my back. After sacrificing everything to get you home, you turn your ass around and go outside unsupervised. Fuck the fact that I distinctly told you no and gave you a valid ass reason why. This is the shit that I was concerned about before we ever made this shit official.

You're not ready for the way I rock. My life and my business are on the line with every decision that we make. I'm out day in and day out trying to find that nigga Benito. I chopped that nigga Hector into small pieces and mailed it to his bitch house behind fucking with you! Not one minute have I stopped and complained about the four holes in me that haven't fully healed, or the painful ass lung that I'm sure is on the verge of collapsing again. Right now, we can't worry about hurt fucking feelings! We've been hit from all angles from people that were supposed to be down for us. I'm sorry, Princess. I can't baby you or pacify your feelings. If you want this shit to work, you need to boss the fuck up. I don't have time for this weak bitch shit. I got niggas to murk and bricks to sell! Instead, you got me out here looking for your ass only to find a nigga in your face trying to get some pussy! God only knows what would have happened had I not showed up. You see what the fuck happens when you go against what the fuck I say!"

"If I had known that I was going to be under a dictator, I would have stayed with Lucifer!"

"Don't ever mention that fuck nigga name in my presence! The difference between him and me is that nigga passed that good ass pussy around, and I want that shit to myself! Let some stupid shit fly out your mouth like that again, and I'll send you to be with him. Since you feel like you under a dictatorship, don't worry about me saying shit to you. Take your stupid ass out there and get kidnapped again, just leave Sophia and Baby Herc here! I'm good on you."

He brushed past me and walked out the door. I knew I should have probably gone behind him, but my body couldn't move. The way he spoke to me crushed my soul. My tears were flowing like a river, and I couldn't contain myself. I started to cry so bad that I felt like I was hyperventilating. Wrapping myself up in the towel, I climbed up in the bed and cried my heart out. I didn't mean to make him think I couldn't handle life with him because I know that I can. Do I have shit to learn? Yes, I do. From the bottom of my heart, I never meant him any harm. I just wanted to get my daughter back, and I will never apologize for that. However, I am sorry because he was hurt and almost lost his life. I don't blame anyone for my being kidnapped but Hector.

I'm lying here crying and feeling like a little girl that's being punished. It's a scene that I've relived for a long time. I should have known this shit wouldn't end well for me. There is no way God would bless me with such a perfect life. I was born to suffer, and I'm over it. It's like I take ten steps forward to be knocked back nine.

Just knowing that he feels this way makes me regret allowing him to make the decision for me to move in here. Neither of us was prepared because we didn't know each other. Out of lust, we jumped head first into the unknown. The more I think, the more I realize his life was much better before I arrived. Tomorrow was going to be the first day of the rest of my life, but first I'm about to cry like a fucking baby. This shit hurts my heart so much.

THE NEXT DAY I woke up still in my feelings but refreshed. Before climbing out of bed to start my day, I made a decision to speak Herc as an adult. He was right. It was time for me to boss up, not to mention take control of my life. I had to admit it, but I had been weak. All I've ever known how to be was what other people wanted me to be. I had no idea who Princess Delgado was. In order for me to find myself, I needed to do it on my own, not under anyone else's direction.

After getting dressed, I said a prayer as I headed to talk with

Hercules. I found him out by the pool chilling. *Why did this man have to be so fine?* I thought to myself. I stood over him trying to find the courage to say what I knew was going to kill my soul afterwards.

"Can I help you with something?" he gritted. I tried my best to keep it together without stuttering or crying. He was being really mean, and it was making me mad and hurt at the same time.

"I just wanted to say that I'm sorry for being selfish and not considering how things affected you. This whole thing has been a lot on me, and I've just been having a hard time adapting. This last year has been a lot on me. I went from being trafficked to a mom, to being forced to live here, and then kidnapped. I'm trying just trying to find some type of balance and normalcy, which is something I've never experienced. As much as it hurts me to admit, I should have listened to you. We aren't ready to be in a relationship. Right now, I know that I'm not capable of being this boss bitch you desire. Before you met me, life was great. Life was the way you wanted it to be. You had Bleu, Miami, and the kids under one roof with no issues. Once I came here shit went sour. Blessing my womb with your seed was the greatest gift you ever could have given me. At the same time, it has caused so much drama for you.

We rushed into this too fast, and that's why we're butting heads now. You told me you weren't relationship material and you had a hard time with commitment. I persuaded you into thinking things would be okay, and I was wrong for that. There is no way I can love you when I've never been loved myself. How can I be the boss bitch you need to be when I don't even have a voice on what I want to do with my life.

One thing I know is that I love you, but I have to love myself first. I know that the best thing for us to do is co-parent. No worries I'm not trying to move out or nothing like that. I made a promise to help you raise Ziyon, and I'm going to do just that. I'll move back to the east wing so that you can have your bedroom to yourself.

"Say less." His lip was curled as he got up from the lawn chair and walked away.

I bit my bottom lip as I tried to hold back the tears. He was being mean for no reason. After gathering myself, I headed back inside the house to cook lunch for the kids. They would be coming back soon from spending the night with Miami.

"Delilah, I was coming in here to cook for the kids." This woman refuses to allow me to cook for the kids.

"It's okay. I just want you to relax. Come on and have a seat so that you can eat some of the lasagna that I made. Ziyon and Brittani have been begging me to cook this. That's why I came and made it for them for lunch."

Sitting down at the table, my stomach growled as she placed a big helping in front of me. I was going to be big as a house if she kept feeding me the way that she has.

"Thank you."

"It's my job. Now eat the food before it gets cold. I have some errands that I need to run. Call me if you need anything."

Delilah was so sweet and made sure to always go above and beyond to make sure we were all straight. She's the best, and I trust her wholeheartedly with my life and the kids.

As soon as I was finished, eating Herc walked inside the kitchen and didn't speak a word to me as he grabbed something to eat.

"Why are you being so mean to me? I'm trying here, Herc?"

"Try harder." He threw the half-eaten lasagna in the sink and walked out of the kitchen.

Now he's the one being a brat, but I wasn't going to kiss his ass period. Instead of sulking, I grabbed the laptop and started searching for GED programs. All I had was a tenth-grade education, so I needed to get my GED. How would I ever teach my kids anything if I didn't know shit? I found an online program that I can do from home and quickly signed up. Hercules could stay in his feelings, but I couldn't stay in mine if I wanted to boss up. I have dreams of doing it real big, and I'll never accomplish my goals if I keep allowing niggas to dictate my moves.

"THANK you so much for keeping the kids for me." Miami and I were lying in my bed catching up on the latest episode of *The Real Housewives of Atlanta*.

"Girl, please! Don't even mention it. I love them. Plus, Baby Herc is preparing me for this little boy I'm about to bring into the world. By the way he an Enfamil bottle away from being the size of Lil Herb and Ari's chunky ass son. That boy is heavy as hell.

"Yes, I don't know what the hell Queenie was feeding my baby while I was gone."

"Queenie took care of him so good, Princess. She has really grown from the drug use. I know she put you through a lot, but I'm also happy you've forgiven her. She's been so happy since she got clean and is able to be in the kids' lives."

"Yeah, I can't believe it, but I'm happy. A year ago, I didn't even think I would ever speak to her again. Now I see her every day. When Herc rescued me from Medellin, my heart melted seeing Queenie. She was crying her heart out. I used to think her ass was heartless, but since she has got clean, I see her in a different life. I'm so thankful that Herc helped her."

A sense of sadness came over me at the very mention of his name. It wasn't supposed to be this way. Our love story isn't supposed to be ending before it ever really got a chance to begin.

"Speaking of Hercules, you had that man on a rampage looking for you yesterday. Do you know he thought Passion did something to you? He went and put a gun in that girl's mouth threatening to blow her brains out. That's how she ended up here with us yesterday. She was able to calm him down and let him know that she had no idea where you were. He scooped her up and grabbed Queenie. We all called your phone, but we didn't get an answer. Where the hell were you?"

"Herc pissed me off, so I went and had a spa day. I just needed to get some air. Things have been really tense around here since I've been back. I became so overwhelmed that I just some time to myself. I would have stayed home had I know it would lead to some damn nigga getting his brains blown out in front of me. Had I known it would lead to us just co-parenting, I never would have gone against his wishes. Shit has been crazy since he brought me here.

Think about it. Before I came, shit was good in this house. Ziyon had both of his parents. You and Brittani were here. The system you guys had worked. One drunk ass fuck in a damn car changed everything for all of us. He thrust me into his world, and I was never ready for it. As I cried myself to sleep last night, I realized that Herc and I don't know anything about each other. He's been my knight in shining armor and always there when I need him. He needed me, and I didn't know. I'm supposed to know when my nigga needs me. I don't even know his favorite color or his favorite food. Please don't tell me what it is. I have so much respect for you, but you're still his ex-wife. Being the new girlfriend and having the ex teach me how to love my nigga is not the business. Don't take that personal. I know you mean well. It's sad to say, but we're no longer a couple. We're just co-parenting and making sure these kids have two parents in this household. It was my decision, but I know that's what I need in order to find me. If I don't start loving me, then how will I ever love him.

"Trust me. I understand, and I don't take it personally. I agree you too did rush into it. At the same time, you guys have to push through this shit. Don't let what happen break you all up. I strongly believe that you two were made for each other. Honestly, I think you're doing the right thing with choosing you. Love you first and him second. If you don't, you'll end up like Bleu, a bitter scorned ass woman who put her all into a nigga that was never going to commit. Herc will respect you more. Trust me. I know. He may be mad at you now, but that shit will eventually subside, and you'll be more in love than ever.

As a word of advice, don't ever do what you did yesterday. It won't do nothing but introduce you to a beast that your beautiful ass is not ready for. You know I'm here if you ever want to talk. In the meantime, handle your shit and boss the fuck up. Let me get home so that I can prepare for this party tomorrow. My brother Gustavo is being released from prison. We're about to do it real big. He and Herc are best friends, so I know he's going to be extremely happy. Make sure you and Passion come through. Y'all ass need to get out and kick it for a change."

"Thanks for the invite. We'll be there. I need to spend some time with her anyway. I know her ass has to be traumatized behind Herc putting a damn gun in her mouth. Why does he have to be so fucking crazy?"

"I've asked myself that for years. See you tomorrow, boo."

Miami climbed out of bed, and I laid there looking at the ceiling. It was lonely lying in bed alone, so I went to gather up the kids to sleep with me. Peeking in on Sophia first, I was taken aback at the scene before me. Herc was sitting in the rocking chair with her on his lap reading a book to her. Sophia was nodding like crazy, but I can tell that she felt so safe with him. Regardless of anything going on between us, I know that he would never hurt her. That's why I'm going to ask him to officially adopt her once we are passed this hump in our relationship. There isn't another man in the world that I would ever allow to raise her.

***

"I'M SO sorry that Hercules did that to you."

"It's okay, Princess. He apologized, and even though I've never had a damn gun put it in my mouth, it showed how far he would go for you. Stop worrying. I am not as fragile as you think."

Passion and I were sitting in the condo chopping it up over mimosas. Queenie had the kids for the day since we were going to be hanging out at Miami's house for her brother's welcome home party.

"I know that you're not fragile. At the same time, you're in a whole new place. All you know is Medellin your ass in Chiraq now. I feel responsible for you, and I would lose my mind if something happened to you. I'm happy you're with me. Honestly, at first, I didn't want anything to do with you. In my opinion, you were with Benito's ass. Then I saw that you were a casualty of our parent's bullshit. It feels so good to have a sister. It was hard being the only child. I used to wish I had a big sister or big brother to keep me company. Queenie used to stress me the fuck out."

I flamed up a blunt and passed it to her.

"Coming here was the best thing that I ever did. All of my life I was lonely and the help basically raised me. My parents loved me through money but kept a tight leash on my ass. So, trust me, I grew up wanting siblings as well. I'm about to live my best life out here. Thank you for allowing me to come and be a part of your family. Don't be mad at Hercules. He apologized once we found out your ass was at the bar drinking. Now let's go. I'm trying to get to this party and have fun, not to mention find me one these fine ass niggas to give pretty babies to."

I choked on the weed smoke hearing her say that. Passion had a sense of humor that was out of this world. As I sat and watched her marvel at herself in the mirror, I took notice of how different she is now than she was back in Medellin. Passion is more alive here in Chicago. I pray that I didn't wake up a sleeping beast because this girl was on one. She was so fucking full of life all of a sudden.

"I'm ready to go too. If I keep drinking these mimosas, I'm going to be fucked up before we even make it."

"You and me both. Hercules is going to go crazy when he sees you with that dress on. You're ass sitting up like some pillows."

Looking in the mirror doing a once over of my outfit, I made my ass cheeks clap. I didn't have any panties on because I definitely wanted to get Herc's attention. He has been avoiding me like the plague. He had no choice but to see me today. I was rocking a blue jean jacket over a hot pink body con dress. Simple diamond studded sandals glistened on my feet. Passion had on the same exact things as me except her dress was lime green. One thing for sure and two for certain we were definitely sisters without a doubt.

SEVEN

MIAMI

The party was in full swing, and I couldn't take my eyes off my little brother Gustavo. He looked so damn good. After doing a five-year bid in federal prison, he was finally out. The nigga was the spitting image of Rio from the television show, *Good Girls,* not to mention touched in the head like him as well. Just looking at him and Herc warmed my heart. They were inseparable growing up, and I know with Gustavo being out, they're about to be right back together.

It was also good to see Diego and my brother getting along. He wasn't too happy about me being with Diego. Somewhere in his mind, he thinks Herc and I will get back together one day, and that will never happen. He must have talked to Herc because all of a sudden he was cool with our relationship. Eventually, he would have had to be cool with it anyway because Diego and I are going to be together.

"This is so nice, Miami." Passion spoke as she poured herself a glass of champagne

"Thank you, boo. Are you enjoying yourself?"

"Trying to. I'm just concerned about Princess. Her ass has been heavily drinking since we made it here. Hercules not talking to her is driving her ass crazy. Looking across the yard, I observed Princess sitting over in a canopy with her eyes trained on Herc. I shook my head because there were a lot of women surrounding him and his crew. Diego was over in the mix with the bitches, but I wasn't an insecure woman. He wasn't a stupid ass nigga either. Diego knows that I will act a fool in this motherfucker, and no one can control me. Passion and I headed over to the canopy and joined her.

"You good, boo?" I asked.

"Yeah, I'm straight. I'm just enjoying this night air. It feels so good. That added with this tequila got me feeling myself. I'm trying to keep calm and not beat this bitch's ass that keeps eyeballing me."

"Don't play that hoe any attention. Trust me. That bitch knows who you are and doing that shit to get under your skin. That's what these thirsty ass bitches do!" Marisol said as she sat next to us.

"Plus, Hercules knows better than to some pull some shit like that while you're here. I don't care if y'all are on a break. He needs to be respectful."

I was getting angry because Herc knows not to invite this bitch A'more to my house anyway. This was the same bitch that kept causing drama for us a while back. He's fucked with her off and on. I actually hadn't seen her around at any functions, so I thought he was done fucking with the bitch."

I kept my game face on pretending not to see this bitch eyeballing Princess. Yeah, this nigga was back fucking A'more with his dumb ass.

"Diego, let me talk to you for a minute!" I yelled across the backyard and headed inside the house.

"Why the hell are you calling me like that?"

"Is Herc fucking that bitch A'more again?"

"Let me get this straight. You called me in here to ask if your ex-husband is fucking somebody?" Without even thinking, I knew that I had fucked up. This really did look fucked up on my part.

"It wasn't like that. I'm just concerned. I don't like the way she was eyeballing Princess."

PRINCESS AND THE PLUG 2 63

"I understand you're concerned for Princess, but she's a grown ass woman. As far as who Herc fucking, that ain't none of my business. As long as he not fucking you, that's all I'm worried about. Stay out of they shit. It's not a good look." He kissed me on the jaw and walked back into the backyard.

More of their associates had started to arrive, and I knew pretty soon they would all be heading down to the club. I was fine with that because I wanted this hoe A'more off the premises. This shit would not end well if I had to fuck her up about Princess. I don't know what it was about that bitch, but Hercules always fucked with her. She's not a regular bitch either. Her father is the mayor. He and Hercules have a lot of ties, so I'm sure that's why he keeps her around. At the same time, he doesn't need to be fucking the bitch. It's bad for business.

"Man, sis! Who is ole girl out there twerking with Marisol in the lime green?"

"That's Princess' sister Passion. She just came here from Medellin."

"You have got to hook me up. She's beautiful ass fuck. That's prime right there. A nigga would love to have her on his arm and his bed."

"No Gustavo. That girl is not ready for a nigga like you. She doesn't need your thuggish ass fucking her head up. It's bad enough Hercules is driving Princess' ass up a wall. I cannot be responsible for you breaking that girl's heart. Plus, Gia is not about to let you be with nobody else."

My brother Gustavo was too fucking gutta for Passion. He would have her ass sitting in the corner pulling out her hair. I didn't want that for her.

"Fuck Gia! That hoe broke bad while I was behind the wall. After doing that bid, sis I'm not trying to go back. A nigga needs to settle down, and from the looks of it, I found my future. Since you won't put me on, I'll put myself on. You're about to have a sister-in-law, and that's on everything."

"Leave that damn girl alone, Gustavo!" I yelled after him, but he paid me no mind. If these Hernandez Cartel niggas thought they were about to stress me out, they had another thing coming.

I HAD FINALLY MADE my last drop for the month, and I was done. Diego no longer wanted me to traffic. I'm almost four months pregnant, and he's done with me doing this shit, which is understandable. Since it was the end of the month, I had to meet up with Herc to go over the month's numbers. I needed to do the numbers so that I could get home and get Brittani to ballet practice. She had been begging to be in the class, and I was against it. I'm an overprotective mother, so all I could think about was her breaking something, and then I would have to break the teacher's ass for letting my baby hurt herself.

I wasn't surprised to see Hercules hard at work when I walked in. That nigga went to sleep counting money and woke up counting the shit.

"Come on. Let's get this over with. Brittani is blowing me up about not being late."

"Hello to you too."

"I'm sorry, Herc. It's just that Brittani says the other girls tease her for being late. I have to get my baby there on time."

Without hesitating, I grabbed the ledger and my money machine to get started.

"Who the fuck is fucking with my baby? I'll shoot a kid behind my kids." I couldn't help but laugh at him because he looked serious as hell.

"Stop it. Brittani can handle her own. I'm glad you had her in boxing early. I told her ass if them bougie ass little girls fuck with her, she better break they shit."

I didn't promote violence or bullying but these kids these days are out of control. If you don't teach children to defend themselves without fear, they can succumb to bullying. Not mine though. I'm beating up the whole family behind my child. Then again, I wouldn't have to because this nutty motherfucker across from me will burn down the whole city behind what belongs to him. That's what I loved most about Hercules. He was very family oriented. That man loves everyone around him whether you're blood or not to the fullest. That is until you cross him. Once you cross him, that's your ass and everybody you love ass.

"Why don't you go ahead and go home. I got this shit here."

"It's cool. You know it will be a while before I'm back working. I need for this pregnancy to be smooth sailing. Plus, I need to talk to you about Princess."

The look on his face told me he didn't want to talk, but I didn't give a fuck.

"What about Princess?"

"You need to leave that bitch A'more alone before Princess finds out about her."

"You don't have anything else better to do besides being in my business?"

"Let's get some shit straight. As long as you're the father of my child, you will always be my business. Because you are my friend, I'm going to call you out on your bullshit. You have Princess walking around feeling like she not good enough for you. That girl feels like she ruined your life. I know you don't feel that way about her. At the same time, you can't want that girl to behave a certain type of way when you're treating her like she's invisible."

"Look, I respect your concern. At the same time, Princess decided she wanted to co-parent, and that's what we're doing,"

"Did you ever stop and think that she said that due to how you talked to her? She's fucked up. Give her a break, Herc?"

"You and I both know that's not how I roll. Princess can't act on emotions and keep thinking she gets a pass because she doesn't know. Princess is not no motherfucking fool. I don't care how mad she gets at me. She has to use common fucking sense. I'm not going to pacify her in regards to that. If she needs this time to find herself, I have to respect that. However, while she finds herself, I still need to move these bricks and make sure I the money flows. As far as A'more goes, that's always business nothing more."

"Keep on being stubborn. Your ass is going to be standing outside the window like Donnell Jones singing while she's on a date with another nigga!"

He was so damn stubborn and arrogant. I tried to give his ass some advice, but men never listened to women. I prayed Princess really did boss up on his ass.

"This is my last time speaking on your relationship. I want to ask you something, and you better tell me the truth."

"What Miami?" He was irritated as hell with me, but I didn't care.

"Do you love Princess?"

"Hell yeah, I love Princess. What type of shit is that to ask me?"

"Then you need to show her. It's okay for you to be soft sometimes. After the way Bleu played you, I feel like it's time to for the commitment. She loves you even though you make it hard. Here, you have to give her a chance."

"I got you man, damn! Can we count this bread so you can take your ass home to Diego?"

I stuck my middle finger up at him and started back counting. I prayed he listened to my advice for a change. Then again, I knew he wouldn't. It would take something drastic for him to get his shit together.

EIGHT

HERCULES

After everything that had transpired my team was solid and back moving weight state to state. I had a solid team and we ready to get back into beast mode. Being shot had slowed me down and lot. A nigga hadn't fully healed, but I was damn near there. I had been shot before, but being hit in your chest was no joke. Besides recovering, I was still on the hunt for Benito's ass. It was as if his ass had vanished off the face of the Earth. He could run, but he definitely couldn't hide. That nigga had to pay the Piper for his treachery. The good thing about that was I had found out where his right hand man Victor Garza was laying his head at.

He has to be the stupidest nigga I ever saw. The bitch ass nigga had been lying low in a safe house out in Winnetka, a small suburb not too far out from Chicago. It wouldn't be too much longer before I found Benito's ass. I couldn't wait to torture that motherfucker. Before I headed out to handle his ass, I needed to make sure my crew knew my expectations. With everything that had happened, I needed to make sure motherfuckers understood that no one was exempt. I was watching everyone like a hawk. I had about twenty of my street soldiers in the building. All of them were little niggas that I had hand-picked over the years. They always handled my shit in the hood. A nigga couldn't step foot on the block without their say so. Their hard footwork is how we found out the whereabouts of Victor Garza. With this newly assembled team, I know shit will go smooth, and we're going to make more money than ever before. Since Benito wanted to play with me, I took every brick he had in his home and all the bread that I could find. I'm not a thief. However, I believe in hood reparations. He crossed me and touched what the fuck belonged to me. The nigga had to pay for that shit. Taking his shit is only a partial payment. His head on a platter will make us even. I'm out for blood, and I'm not stopping until I get it. These niggas went against the grain and lost. I'm still highly disappointed in Hector. He knew he could never win against me. I can't blame a nigga for trying though.

"This is a new month and new quarter. We did well last month, but this month we need to do great. I'm not taking any shorts or losses so make sure everybody is on their shit. We took hit these past months, but we're back like we never left. As you all know Gustavo is back and jumping right back into his position of running the blocks. Before this meeting is over, every nigga on the street team needs to speak with Gustavo and get new burners. Diego is my right hand and works directly with me. Marisol and Passion are over the girls. Jigg, you now have the pleasure of going state to state with the girls making sure they're safe and ensuring that the product moves according to the routes. With Miami being on maternity leave, Queenie will be picking up all of her duties.

You all already know how this shit goes, so there's no need for me to go into detail. Before I end this meeting though, I want you all to know that I appreciate you all for holding it down for me in my absence. You could have easily switched sides, and you didn't. For that, I'll forever be indebted to you. At the same time don't get it fucked up. If you cross me, I'll murder your entire bloodline. This meeting is dismissed."

Watching everyone disburse, I took notice of Passion. She fit in quite well. Come to find out she knows about some of Benito's associates. With her help, I've been able to acquire all of his business in his absence. At first, I didn't trust her, and I still have my reservations. That's why I have her under the watchful of Marisol and Queenie besides me. I have to keep an eye on both of them. Queenie is still new to this sober lifestyle, and Passion was raised by my enemy. At the same time, she's extremely lucrative and beneficial to my cause.

They've shown me their loyalty, but I don't want to put it all into them quick. Queenie has been holding it the fuck down for The Hernandez Cartel and for that I salute her. Not only that, she's been really helping out with the kids. There was a time when I didn't even trust her to be in the same room as Princess. Now I love when she comes over because Princess enjoys her company. Princess and I might not be on good terms, but I'm proud of myself for at least giving her other reasons to smile.

AFTER A LONG ASS DAY, I just wanted to get home and spend some time with the kids. I had been promising to play Ziyon in *Fortnite,* but by the time I would make it home, he would be asleep. I already had put people on the house Victor where was. That nigga wasn't going anywhere. Loud sounds were coming from the family room. Walking inside, I was surprised to see Princess and Ziyon playing *Fortnite.* Sophia was running around with Bonnie and Clyde playing. They were dropping popcorn everywhere. Baby Herc was fast asleep in his swing. How he was able to sleep through this madness was amazing.

The scene before me is what all men like to come home to after a long hard day of selling bricks. Running a drug empire is just as hard as working a nine to five. Hell, maybe even harder. Dodging them people and trying to stay alive is no punk.

"Look, daddy! Princess is playing *Fortnite* with me." He was so excited and crazy about her. Bleu would never play video games with him. He just seemed so much more alive with Princess in his life.

"I see. I'm glad you're having fun." Removing my suit jacket and loosening my tie, I joined them.

"Here you can play. He's been waiting for you to come home and you definitely need to spend some time with him." Princess handed me the controller and tried to walk away, but I grabbed her.

"Don't leave. We're chilling like a family is supposed to. It's not often I make it home, and everyone is up. Usually, all of you are asleep."

"Well, you need to come home earlier. Come on, Sophia. It's time for a bath."

"Noooo! Da Da!" Sophia wobbled over to me with her bowlegs and climbed in my lap. From the look on Princess' face, I could tell she was taken aback hearing her call me daddy.

"See. Even Sophia wants to stay and kick it with her daddy. Stop being stubborn and come chill with your family."

"I have to get the kitchen in order." She tried to yank away, but I held on to her tighter. Her belly shirt lifted a little, and that's when I notice the tattoo.

"Calm down. I pulled her closer and lowered the top of her pants a little." The tattoo was sexy as hell. You couldn't even tell that there was previously a name there.

"When did you get that?"

"The day I went out without your permission." She rolled her eyes and yanked away from me.

Princess was really being stubborn at this point. She quickly walked out of the family room, and I didn't try and stop her that time. It's like as soon as she was gone Baby Herc woke up screaming hollering. Imagine me trying to calm him down, play *Fortnite* with Ziyon, love on Sophia, and pay attention to Bonnie and Clyde. No wonder Princess be asleep when I come home.

AFTER A GOOD TWO hours of spending time with the kids, they were all asleep. A nigga needed a fat ass blunt.

"You look lost. This is the East wing."

"Nah! I'm not lost. I'm exactly where the fuck I'm supposed to be. I know you mad at a nigga but cut all that shit out. That attitude is not even you, Princess. I'm so serious right now. Put that computer away and come get lifted with a nigga.

"I'm studying, Herc. I take this GED test in a week, and I don't want to fail." She ran her hands over her face in frustration, and that made me feel kind of fucked up. I knew this shit between us was probably fucking with her mental. At that moment, I knew I needed to take the high road. She was driving herself crazy trying to be strong for herself and hold the household down trying to prove a point to me. That's not how I want shit to be. Coming in the house today and seeing my family made me see things in a different light. That with the look on her face hearing Sophia call me daddy for the first time was priceless. As much as I wanted to keep applying pressure to her, she didn't deserve that. I've been coming home nightly and checking on her before I even lay it down. She's been falling asleep studying. I admired her drive more than she would ever know. I could very well fall back and let her work hard and trying to be better woman, but she didn't deserve that. The boss ass nigga in me couldn't even let my baby suffer like that any longer. As fucked up in the head as I had been in my heart lately, I knew all I wanted was Princess.

"For real. Take a break. You look frustrated as fuck. Puff on this while I run you some bath water."

"I can't take a break."

"You can and you will. I'm not about to argue with your stubborn ass." She was really being difficult rolling her eyes and shit.

Heading into the bathroom, I cut the hot water and threw some of the bath bombs in it she likes. A bath wasn't shit without candles, so I found some and lit them. Lately, she had started sipping on wine and different shit like that. I grabbed her bottle of some of our best Chardonnay from the wine cellar. After pouring her a huge glass, I rolled up a fat ass blunt she could smoke by herself. Walking back into the room, I could tell she still wanted to have an attitude with a nigga. Grabbing her hand, I led her into the bathroom and sat on the side of the tub.

"What are you doing, Hercules?"

"Just let me do me." I removed her shirt and then her yoga pants. For the first time, I was able to see her tattoo in full view."

"Do you like it?"

"I love it. That's the best thing you could have ever done."

I grabbed her hand and helped her inside the tub. Before leaving out the bathroom, I handed her the wine and the blunt that I rolled for her. Instead of sticking around the bedroom, I headed to the west wing where I had been staying. I decided to take a shower to relieve some of the stress of the day away. Besides trying to make shit right with Princess, I was getting stressed not knowing this nigga Benito whereabouts. The last thing I needed was for him to get a chance to hurt Princess again. Now that Passion has gone against him, I'm sure he's gunning for her too. That nigga cannot get another one up on me. I simply can't go out like that.

After showering, I stepped out and wrapped a towel around my waist. I wasn't sleeping in the west wing alone. Princess was sleeping next to me whether she wanted to or not. It was a good thing she was drying off when I made it back to the east wing. Without hesitation, I picked her up and threw her up over my shoulder.

"Ahhhhh! What are you doing, Herc?"

"Shut that shit up! I'm about to fuck the shit out you." I smacked her on the ass as hard as I could.

Once I made it back to the west wing, I threw her on the bed. Letting the towel drop from my waist, I wasted no time climbing on top of her. Princess' pussy was soaking wet, so it didn't take no time for me slide in. It had been so long since I felt the inside of her a nigga was definitely going to nut quick.

"We're going to make this work right!" I roughly entered her, and she let out a loud gasp.

The way she wrapped her legs around my waist and pulled me closer lets me know she missed this dick just as much. As soon as I was getting ready to nut, Princess rolled me over and mounted me. During the times we did have sex, I was always in control, and I could tell she was afraid to be free, so seeing her in this light made a nigga take notice that she really had been holding back. She grabbed my hands and placed them above my head as she rode my dick as if she was trying to prove a point. The fact that she was staring me in my eyes the whole time had me wondering what the fuck she was thinking. Princess was riding the fuck out of me and had me bussing nuts like a bitch.

"Ahhhhh!" she screamed out as I felt her juices running all over my dick and down my legs.

Once she was finished, I thought she would roll over and lay beside me. Instead, she grabbed the towel and wrapped it around her body before walking out of the room. I jumped up and went after her.

"Where are you going? I told you I wanted you to sleep with me."

"Nah! I'm good. I'll go sleep in the east wing, and you stay over here."

"Come on now, Princess. A nigga is trying to make shit right with us. Why are you making it so fucking difficult for me?" She was still walking and refusing to turn back around and look at me. Once she made it back to the room, she flamed up a blunt that was sitting on the nightstand. I swear she had been smoking more than I had ever seen before this shit happened to her

"Let's get some shit straight! I'm not Bleu!"

"I know you're not Bleu! What the fuck are you talking about?"

"I'm talking about you thinking that I'm about to settle for this wishy-washy ass behavior. What you're not going to do is go fuck that hoe and then come lay up with me? I don't give a fuck if its business or personal. I'm not accepting any other bitch, period. Bleu laid up in this house, held you down, and allowed you to fuck other bitches simply so she can have a piece of you in her life. It drove her crazy, and that will never be me. If you want me to boss up, you have to be fully committed to us. Now when I say committed, that means more than just being faithful. It also means removing all doubt about us being together. If you don't fully think we should be in a relationship, then we don't need to. I want to lie beside you and know that you believe in us as much as I do. Any relationship filled with doubt is a waste of fucking time. Hercules, I've been through enough, and I can't take it anymore. I'm trying my best to live here and keep the family together. Ziyon and Brittani love me. Hearing Sophia call you daddy tonight made tears come to my eyes. Our bond has strengthened with the birth of our son. What these people have tried to do to us can't break the family we've built. Instead of us walking around trying to figure out ways to co-parent, we need to be figuring out ways to protect our family. The ball is in your court, Hercules. I've laid my cards on the table."

Princess had rendered me speechless and confirmed to me in making the right decision that I was about to make. Instead of responding to her, I rushed into the walk-in closet and grabbed the gift that I had been hiding from her. I laughed silently listening to her smack her lips and mumble underneath her breath. Her ass wasn't going to be talking that shit in a minute though. Once I grabbed what I was I looking for I walked back in the room to see Princes wiping her eyes.

"What are you crying for?"

"I'm not crying, Hercules." She was wiping her eyes as she spoke.

"Yes, your tough ass is, but I have something that will make you smile. After you gave birth to our son, I really wanted to do something really special for you. While I was planning, you were kidnapped, and I got hit up. When I woke up, I promised myself that if I got you back, I would make you the happiest woman alive. It's taken a lot of soul searching for me to do this because I never want to hurt you. I've always put my drug empire in front of my relationships, but I want to be able to make them both a priority. I know that with you I can do that. Coming home tonight and seeing you so invested with being a mother was everything to me. I guess what a nigga trying to say is I want to give you the commitment that you deserve. Princess Delgado, will you do me the honor of rocking a nigga's last name?"

I flipped open the small engagement and showed her the hugest rock she probably had ever seen. I wasn't no traditional ass nigga so all that getting on one knee shit wasn't me. I was doing the shit my way.

"Yes, I would love to rock your last name." Princess grabbed me tightly by the face and kissed me passionately.

Picking her up bridal style I carried her back to the west wing where the fuck she belonged. For the rest of the night, we made love like we never had before. For that short period of time, it was only the both of us that mattered. Nothing else going on even mattered. I just wanted to focus on my future wife.

THE NEXT DAY I woke up to Princess, Queenie, Miami, Marisol, and Passion all in the kitchen discussing the wedding. I wanted no parts of the shit. Money was no object, and we had no budget. Just tell me what the colors are, and I'll be there. I would leave the logistics up to her. At first, I had all intentions on heading to handle the nigga Victor Garza, but I needed to handle this shit with A'more. For years, we had been fucking off and on. She was like something to do when there was nothing to do, or in my case just having my cake and eat it too. The way Princess put her foot down last night, I know for a fact that she was not playing with a nigga. I can't afford to lose my family over no bitch. A'more was the daughter of the mayor, but the way she carried herself behind closed doors one would never know. She reminded me of that bitch Pandora from the movie *Baby Boy*. She was a freak ass hoe with connections, so I always kept this dick in her life. That added with the fact that I could call her when shit got real and she would be down.

Before I could even get into her house good, she was opening the door. She had on a sheer pink robe with nothing underneath.

"Since when you start calling before you come? I'm used to you being over here in bed waiting on me to get home from the office."

"Yeah. This not that type of visit."

"Well, what type of visit is it, Hercules?" She sat across from me and folded her legs waiting for me to speak.

"Look, this shit between us has to come to an end. I'm getting ready to get married to my son's mother Princess, and I'm not trying to go into the marriage on some fucked up shit."

"Hercules, I'm not in the mood for the bullshit today."

"I don't give a fuck what you not in the mood for! It is what the fuck it is. Our personal relationship is over. I'll pay you more every month going forward in regards to our business affairs. Just respect the fact that Princess is my fiancée."

"Whatever you say, Hercules. Let yourself out."

She was obviously in her feelings, but I didn't give a fuck. A'more knew about Princess from the jump, so it's not like she didn't know who she was. She shouldn't even be in her feelings about me getting married. A'more could never handle being with a nigga like me.

"AHHHHHHH!"

This nigga Victor was crying out like a bitch each and every time I shot a nail into his foot. Gustavo and I had been torturing the fuck out of this nigga for hours, and he was not giving up Juan or shall I say Benito. I'm still fucked up in the head behind that nigga pulling that snake shit off. I have to give it to him because I never saw the shit coming.

"I'm going to ask you one more motherfucking time! Where the fuck is Benito?"

"I don't know. He's been missing since he left Cuba! If I knew, I would tell you. Please let my wife go!" he cried, and I fell out laughing. I didn't give a fuck about his wife.

"You think I give a fuck about that bitch! Did you give a fuck about mine while you were following her and taking pictures of her? I should let my nigga right here fuck the lining out her old pretty ass and make your bitch ass watch!"

Gustavo was across the room holding a gun to his wife's head making her watch him get fucked up.

"Please let her go! It's me you want."

He was crying like the bitch ass nigga he was. The crazy part about all of this is that he helped kidnap Princess with a smile. He might care about his wife, but I don't. The bitch is a casualty of war at this point.

"If you love your wife like you say you do, then you'll tell me where the fuck Benito is at?"

"I told you I don't know!" This nigga had mustered up some courage to raise his damn voice at me, and he had sealed his wife fate.

"Put a bullet in that bitch's head!" Without hesitation, Gustavo shot that bitch in her head, and she instantly dropped to the floor.

"Noooooo! She didn't have anything to do with this!" He was beside himself at this point and crying uncontrollably.

"You ever heard of guilty by association? That goes for your bitch too! For the sake of your kids having at least one parent, I'm going to do you a solid. I'll let you live if you at least tell me why? What made Benito pop up out of the blue and all of a sudden want to kidnap his daughter? Why did you motherfuckers try and kill me?"

It was obvious he wasn't going to tell me where the fuck Benito was. Maybe after seeing his wife's brains being blown out, he would say something.

"You have no idea at all. This shit is bigger than Benito. He was what you call a casualty of war. Humberto Hernandez can tell you better than I ever can. Let me give you a word of advice before you kill me. Blood is not always thicker than water young blood!" Without hesitation, I grabbed my gun from my waist and emptied every bullet in his ass.

"Did he just say the name he thought I said?" Gustavo inquired.

"I don't want to talk about it. Get this shit cleaned up, and we'll meet back up later. Don't say shit to Miami about this. I don't need her asking me a million questions or being worried about me. If she knows about this, then she will go and talk to Princess. My baby's been through enough. I just want her to be able to plan her wedding with no issues."

I was fucked up in the head by the name this nigga had just revealed.

"I got you bro, but we need to figure this shit out. This shit is crazy, and we need to handle all these motherfuckers immediately. I would ask you how you feel right now, but I already know. Just hit me if you need me." We dapped it up and got the fuck up out there.

As I jumped on the highway to head home, I couldn't understand why my father is behind all of this. On paper, he's supposed to be dead. At least that's how we made it look. To know that he is behind the attempt on my life makes this shit worse. We had a motherfucking deal, and he had reneged. I think I already know where the fuck to find him, but I still need to find Benito's ass. For him to kidnap his own daughter and plan that elaborate façade with me, there has to be a good reason. My mind was so fucked up behind this that I drove around aimlessly trying to make sense of it all. I just couldn't wrap my mind around the shit, but I was definitely going to get down to the bottom of it. If my father thought that he was going to come out of retirement and take over everything that I've built for this family, he has another fucking thing coming. Right about now, I need my mother here for some type of advice. Had his ass did what the fuck he was supposed to do as the head of the family, we wouldn't even be here.

––––––––

AN HOUR LATER, I was pulling into the driveway. Princess was going to be pissed because I missed our son's doctor appointment. On the drive home, I remembered that I missed it. She had told me at the last minute, but I promised I would make it on time.

Walking inside of the bedroom, Princess was knocked out. It was a couple of days before she had to take her GED, and she was studying harder than ever. Getting undressed, I climbed in bed next to her and laid my head on her chest. This was one night that I needed to feel some warmth and real love. At this point, all I had in this world was Princess. She was all the family I had, and it was fucked up.

"WAKE up Hercules so that you can eat?" Sitting up I looked at Princess standing over me with a tray full of food. For a minute, I thought I was crazy because it was five in the morning.

"Princess, why are you up this early like this? It's not daylight yet."

"Because I had to beat Delilah to it. Every morning I want to get up and cook for the kids, and she beats me to it. Well, I beat her to it this time. I made you a chorizo omelet with smothered potatoes and toast."

Princess looked like she was so happy to feed a nigga. It was actually cute. It was early as fuck, and I wanted to go back to sleep, but my stomach started to growl looking at the plate.

"This looks so good. Thank you, babe. I'm sorry I missed his doctor appointment. Shit got hectic out there in the streets. I'll make it up to you."

"It's okay. One thing for sure and two for certain I know that you would never miss anything intentionally. One thing I want you to know is that I can handle certain things on my own when it comes to the kids and things that need to get taken care of around the house. I'm not one of those needy ass women who can't function without their nigga. You can run the streets and do what you have to do. I'll be right here waiting."

I was once again rendered speechless hearing her speak like that.

It's not often you come across a woman who is not afraid to get the job done on her own.

"That's real, and I appreciate it." She leaned over, kissed me on the lips, and climbed up in bed with me. Silence filled the room as I stuffed my face and she scrolled through her phone.

"Do you like it?"

"I love it. This shit is so good that I might have to tell Delilah to let you cook my breakfast from now on."

"Now you know she's not going for that. She doesn't even want me to cook for the kids. Let her tell it I don't feed Baby Herc enough, or I don't eat enough fruit. Do you know she makes me fruit platters every day?"

I was finished with the food, so she grabbed the tray and sat it on the dresser. Princess was on point this morning because she had my cold bottle of water and my blunt ready. Fuck food being a way to a nigga's heart. Just have my blunt already rolled, and I'll love you forever.

"That's Delilah for you. She has worked for me for many years, and I never thought I would have to share her the way I do now. She takes care of you and the kids better than me. I'm happy about that because I can trust her with my family. You and the kids are precious cargo, and I have to protect y'all at all cost. You know its people in this world that want me dead simply because I'm successful at shit that they aren't. This shit with Hector, Bleu, and your father has me not trusting a soul."

"Do you trust me?" Princess straddled me.

"If I didn't trust you, I never would have proposed. You're the only thing in my life that makes sense right now."

She bent down and kissed me on the lips followed by a trail of kisses down my chest. Princess was tugging at my boxers, and I knew what she was trying to do, so I stopped her.

"What the hell is the problem, Hercules? Why every time I try to suck your dick, you stop me? I bet you don't stop that bitch when she is doing it." Princess jumped out of bed and rushed inside the bathroom. She slammed it so hard she made my ass jump.

I ran my hand over my face in frustration with her. Instead of blowing up, I smoked my blunt to calm down. The sound of her sniffling made me jump up and burst in the bathroom. She was sitting on the toilet seat with her head down.

"Really Princess? I know you not in here crying cause I won't let you suck my dick."

"I'm not crying."

I walked inside the bathroom and kneeled in front of her. I didn't know if I should be laughing at this crazy ass girl or feeling good as fuck. I've never had a woman cry about giving me head. The shit beyond me, but I have my reasons.

"Yes, the fuck you are. Come here. Let me talk to you because I think you're thinking about this all wrong."

I grabbed her by the hand, but her ass was reluctant to move. I had to damn near yank her arm out of socket pulling her into the bedroom.

"It's cool, Hercules. I understand." I kneeled in front of her and lifted her chin so that she could look at me in my eyes. She needed to truly understand where I was coming from.

"No, you don't understand because if you did you wouldn't be sitting here acting like this. You haven't done anything wrong, so stop thinking that. As far as another woman goes, I'm not going to even address that shit. You mean more to me than anything in this world, so any other bitch is irrelevant. Do you actually think that I wouldn't want them pretty ass lips wrapped around my dick? Hell yeah! I would love that, but you've been through a lot with men making you do things that dehumanized you. I just never want to make you feel like you're less than a woman by performing sexual acts like that on me. Sometimes I feel like I have to hold back in an effort not to make you feel disrespected sexually."

"Oh my god, Hercules! Let's end this shit right here. Stop feeling like I've been through so much that I'm fragile. You don't have to hold back when it comes down to sex with me, not that you do because you be drilling all up in this pussy, and we have a damn baby to prove it. Despite the hiccups we've been through, you've always treated me better than any man that I've ever been with.

Herc, I don't think you understand just how good to me you are. My momma named me Princess, but you make me feel like a queen. For that alone, I love you more than life itself.

Baby, you have to understand the difference in something being taken away from me and me giving myself to you. Those men were forced upon me sexually. I want you to make love to me in every position possible and fuck my brains out whenever you see fit. My wanting to give you head is just what I want to do to please you as your woman.

You tossed and turned all night so, I knew something happened yesterday that had your soul troubled. Instead of me nagging and asking questions, I decided to cook you breakfast and suck that dick. Stop viewing me as the woman who was weak and sexually abused. Start viewing me as the strong black queen that's getting ready to rock your last name and give you all the babies you want."

"I never looked at it that way. I apologize if I made you feel that way. Going forward, I'm not letting up when I'm in that pussy."

"Yayyyy me! Now sit down so that I can show you what this mouth do."

Princess pushed me back on the bed and dropped down to her knees. I don't even remember shit else. Her head game was so damn vicious the shit had me in a trance. If I wasn't gone off the pussy, then I definitely was gone off her mouth. Lil baby was the total package all the way around. I now understand why she was so lucrative to Lucifer's organization for all of those years.

AFTER PRINCESS and I fucked a couple of more times, I headed to see Queenie. It was imperative that she and I had a sit-down. For some reason, I feel like she can be a key factor in helping me find Benito so that I could get down to the bottom of what the fuck my father wants. Just thinking about his ass pisses me off. My mother had been dead for well over a year, and he didn't attend the services, didn't send condolences, and the nigga didn't even check to see if I was okay. No one would ever think that at one time we were a happy, successful family. He ruined that shit, and all of a sudden, he wants to come back and fuck up my happy family.

"What's up, Hercules? I'm clean, and I haven't done shit."

"Calm down, Queenie. I know that you've been doing a phenomenal job with everything. I came over to talk to you about something."

She stepped to the side and let me inside her townhome. She had finally given up her house in the hood. Looking around, I was impressed. Queenie had damn good taste.

"Is everything okay with you and Princess?"

"Yeah. We're good. Everything is good on the home front. I actually came over here to ask you some questions in regards to Benito.

"I can't wait until you find that nigga. Please call me, Hercules. I want in on the torture. He made my life a living hell, and I plan on being there to send him to hell. That man really forgot who the fuck I was around this motherfucker."

"I need you to tell me this nigga's history in the Chi. Like who he was back in the day when y'all was running shit. I have reason to believe that he and my father are in on this shit together."

I didn't go into detail about what Victor had divulged to me, or the fact that he was dead. Some shit didn't need to be said. The less these motherfuckers know, they can't tell on you. Now Queenie is as solid as they come, but after what the fuck I had just been through, a nigga had to move cautiously.

"Who is your father? I thought you said your father had died and left everything to you."

"His name is Humberto Hernandez, and due to unfortunate circumstances, we had to make it look like he died. Years ago, he made some bad business decisions and fucked over some people. My mother and sister Hermina were kidnapped, raped, and tortured for weeks until he paid the money he fucked up. My mother survived, but my sister didn't. She was only sixteen, and they basically raped and tortured her to death. I've never spoken about my sister to anyone outside of our family. No one really knew about her because she had Down Syndrome. My father was ashamed of her, so he kept her hidden inside the house.

At the time, I was only sixteen years old. Once my mother was rescued, and we found out the real circumstances behind the shit, I knew I had to step up. My uncles Dario and Naldo forced him to step down from his faction. It was then that I was placed in his seat. For years, they groomed me for when I would take over. I just never imagined it would be so soon. Not too long after my mother was rescued and my father had stepped down, we found out that he was behind the shit. He had been stealing from his own brothers, and in an effort to get the money he owed back to them, he had his own daughter and wife kidnapped. The nigga is such a fucking snake that he was trying to have his brothers pay a ransom to him so that he could pay them back their own damn money.

Once my uncles got wind of the shit they wanted him gone permanently. They couldn't bring themselves to actually kill him, so they made it look like he died in a plane crash. After that, my uncles decided to hand over the Hernandez Cartel to me. They then retired to Amsterdam and have never returned. As long as I give them their proper cut every month, we're good. I've been running this shit for the last ten years without any bullshit, and now he wants to show and bring me down. He was supposed to be in Casablanca and never to return to Chicago. Apparently, he has different plans."

I didn't even mean to go that far with my family business, but it actually felt good to get it off of my chest. I had never spoken a word about any of this to anyone. Observing Queenie flame up a cigarette and pace back forth let me know she knew my father.

"We worked for Humberto. That's how we flooded the streets with bricks back then. Every brick that was sold in the Midwest came through him. Hearing about his brothers and a damn cartel is all new to me. I knew he was what they considered the plug, but that's all I knew. I only met him once, so I knew nothing about him or his family. Him, Benito, and Victor Garza all had dealings."

"Okay. What happened that sent Benito to jail?"

"Shit was cool. I was his ride or die bitch, and the nigga gave me the world. We were like hood royalty, and of course, bitches hate that. I thought I had a solid, faithful, paid ass nigga. All along this nigga was a cold ass liar. I went on a run out of town to transport for him. When I made it back to the house we shared, he was fucking a bitch in the bed we shared. One thing led to another, and I lost control. Without thinking, I grabbed his gun and shot her. Without hesitation, he fucked me up and put me out of the house. A couple of days later, I find out he was in jail and charged with her murder.

Everything went downhill from there. A month after him being locked up, I found out I was pregnant. During the entire pregnancy, I stood by him. All of a sudden, everybody was being picked up across the city. They were calling him a rat, but I knew he wasn't built like that. He portrayed himself to be a gangsta ass nigga that went by the street code. Everybody that once fucked with us because I held him down ostracized me. I was no longer a part of everything that we built. The entire time I was pregnant and going back forth to court, visiting him in jail, and making sure those books stayed full. I gave birth to Princess about a month after he was found guilty. I took her to see him, and he went ballistic because I had his daughter at a prison. He forbid me to ever come back, and I was never to bring Princess back there. For months, I went crazy sending letters, and he never wrote back. Pretty soon I couldn't take it anymore and started using. Shit went downhill for me from that point on.

Now I find out that nigga was never who he said he was. Come to find out he was released after a couple of months of being sentenced. How in the fuck does that happen unless he was a rat? Either that or the government is behind the shit. How does one get sentenced to life, then let out of prison, and there are no records of him ever being in the prison system.

All of this time that nigga has been in Medellin living the life with his other family. Imagine finding out that he has been in his other daughter's life since birth, not to mention married. He had been married the entire time we were fucking around. He used me to traffic here in the states and tricked the fuck out of me. At first, I was hurt, but now I'm angry behind him hurting my daughter. What so good about Passion that he didn't fuck with Princess? Even though I was fucked up to her. He should have been here to take care of her when I couldn't."

Queenie's face was now full of tears, and it was hard for me to see her like that. How ironic is it that both Princess' father and my father were fucked up individuals.

"Don't trip, Queenie. I promise you gone get your payback. That's my word. Do you know anywhere Benito could be?"

"Nope. He had no family here. If you find Victor, I'm positive he will lead you to Benito. Now that's enough about all of this bullshit. What's on the agenda for Princess' birthday tomorrow? I've ordered the dopest birthday cake for her.

"Her birthday is tomorrow?" My ass was feeling stupid because I remember her telling me when her birthday was, but it slipped my mind. The crazy part was that she hadn't spoken on it at all.

"Don't tell me you forgot, Herc?"

"Honestly, I did. Don't worry though. She's going to have the best birthday party a princess could ever have. Here go shopping and get you some fly shit to wear to her white and gold affair tomorrow night at King's Palace."

I handed Queenie some bread and rushed out of her house. My ass had less than twenty-four hours to put a birthday party together and make sure the city showed up and showed out for my baby.

NINE

PRINCESS

"Please don't let me fall, Hercules!" This nigga had me walking through the house with a damn blindfold on. As he guided me down the stairs, I was so afraid he was going to let me fall that I was shaking.

"Put one foot in front of the other, Princess. You make this spontaneous shit hard on a nigga."

"I'm sorry, babe. You're high, and I'm scared you're going to make me fall."

"The only fall I've ever allowed you to take was falling for a real nigga. Okay, we've just made it to the last step. Step down, and then we're heading out of the door."

I was trying my best not to be overexcited, but I couldn't wait to see what Hercules had gotten me. It had been years since I celebrated my birthday. It literally slipped my mind. I knew it was a birthday surprise, and I was thirsty to see what it was.

"Can I take the blindfold off now?"

"Slow down. I'm about to take it off."

I rubbed my hands together in anticipated as he removed it. My eyes got wide as saucers looking at a black on black 2019 Rolls Royce Wraith. It was draped in a big ass red bow.

"Ahhhhhh!" I screamed and jumped all over Herc. A while back, he asked me what my dream car was, and I told him. I can't believe this nigga had got me a fucking Wraith.

"Happy Birthday, Princess." He handed me the key fob, and I kissed him all over his face before rushing to see the inside. The leather was so fucking soft and pretty.

"Come on, Herc! Let's take it out for a test drive." I was so excited to see how smooth it drove.

"Later Princess. Right now, you have to get ready for your birthday. You have a glam squad on the way."

Tears welled up in my eyes listening to Herc. He was really going out of his way to make my day special. I closed my car door and damn near ran into his arms.

"Thank you so much. I've never had a birthday party before." I was doing that ugly girl cry and wetting his silk shirt all up.

"Wipe your face. This is the first of many birthday parties with me. If you want to, I'll throw you a party every month to make up for the ones you didn't have. I love you and today is all about you. Now stop this crying shit and get dressed. We're about to fuck the city up the Hernandez way!"

He kissed me passionately and smacked me on the ass as I rushed into the house to get dressed. Outside of the birth of my children, this was the best day of my life.

MY PARTY WAS at one of the hottest clubs in Chicago. If you weren't a heavy hitter, you definitely couldn't even grace the doors. I was in awe of all the strippers swinging from the ceilings doing tricks and shit. I swear there was so much money being thrown that it was ridiculous. The DJ was on point and made sure to shout out Herc and how it was his fiancée's birthday. The love I was receiving was everything. I smiled looked at Herc and his crew going hard with the strippers and popping bottles.

"Bitch! This party so lit!" Passion yelled as she smacked me on the ass. I couldn't do nothing but bend over and start twerking. On cue, the DJ started playing "Act Up" by City Girls. Every bitch in the club was going crazy.

Real Ass Bitch Give A Fuck About A Nigga
Real Birkin Bag, Hold five or six figures
Stripes on my ass so he calls this pussy Tigger
Fucking on a scamming ass, rich ass nigga!

"YASSSSSS!" I screamed out, and that's when I felt cold steel underneath my short ass dress. Quickly turning around, I grabbed my chest when I turned around and realized it was Herc.

"I'm about to let a round off in your pussy if you don't sit the fuck down Princess. Why the fuck you ain't got no panties on?" Herc gritted.

"I can't wear panties with this dress, Hercules!"

"Then I suggest you sit the fuck down or go over in your private section and shake your ass over there. You're up in this bitch dancing with your ass all out letting these niggas see what the fuck belongs to me. I don't care if it is your birthday. You are marrying a rich ass nigga and them City Girl bitches scam rich niggas. Y'all are not the same."

I rolled my eyes at Herc because he was being so damn dramatic. He wasn't about to blow my high at all. I didn't want to argue, so I went back to the section and sat down. Marisol, Miami, and my mother were sitting around getting fucked up, minus Miami of course.

Looking over at my sister, I noticed that she was looking sad.

"What's wrong with you? Your ass was just turning up and now you looking like somebody died."

I followed her eyes, and I noticed she was looking at Gustavo. He had his face buried in some stripper's big ole ass booty. The bitch had a ridiculous ass wagon she was dragging. How in the fuck does she get around with that thing? The hoe has got to have serious back pains.

"I'm good, sis."

I knew she was lying as she turned up the bottle of Ace of Spades. Her ass had become a party animal since coming to Chicago. Now that she was fucking with Gustavo, she was off the chain. That added with making money for the cartel, the bitch had lost all sense. Passion didn't even have to work for Hercules. She had money put away that she could live off of. This shit was simply for the thrill. That's what happens to sheltered kids. When you let they ass out, they go wild, and that's exactly what her ass was doing. I was going to let her live her best life as long as her life isn't in jeopardy. I pray Gustavo doesn't hurt her because these niggas out here were savage.

"Happy Birthday, baby. I'm going to go ahead and head to the house. Miami is not feeling good, so I'm going to drop her off then head home. I love you, and I'm so happy you're enjoying your day."

"Thank you so much for coming, and I love my MAC cosmetics themed cake." Queenie kissed me and walked out of the section.

"Happy Birthday, boo. Don't get too drunk. I would stay longer, but I don't feel good for some reason. Don't tell Diego because he will want to leave, and I want him to have fun for a change. I'll call you tomorrow and sit your ass down before Herc shoot up the place." I laughed, and Miami and I exchanged hugs before she left.

Looking over at Marisol, this bitch was so high that she was dosing off. I just shook my head. Her ass will go to sleep anywhere. Who in the fuck goes to sleep in a loud ass club?

"I'll be back, Passion. I have to go to the bathroom."

I quickly rushed from the section to the bathroom. I was thanking God that it wasn't a line as I rushed into the stall. After pissing, I washed my hands and headed out the door. Not really paying attention, I ended up bumping into someone.

"Princess!"

Taking a good look at the guy, my heart raced as I realized who it was. It was this big nigga named Giovanni that always requested me when I was with Lucifer. This nigga was a nasty motherfucker and just looking at him makes my skin crawl.

"Oh hey," I stammered and tried to walk away quickly, but he pulled me back. I immediately yanked away from his ass. My heart started to speed up as he held me so close to him.

"I would love one of those golden showers right about now!"

"We got a problem, my nigga!" Hearing Herc's voice made my heart drop. This was always my biggest fear. Why did this shit have to happen on today of all days?

"Nah Herc! We don't have a problem. I was just trying to fuck up some commas on this bad bitch right here. Her pussy and head game so official. If she weren't a pass around, I would have wifed her beautiful ass up a long time ago." He licked his lips and walked in the bathroom like it was nothing.

"I'm sorry, Herc."

His face had embarrassment, shame, and anger written all over it. He didn't even respond. He just walked away from me. He didn't even go back to the section. That nigga walked out of the club and left my ass— that hurt more than anything in this world. Walking back toward the section, I saw everybody leaving out.

"Where y'all going?" Asking Diego like I didn't know why.

"The club is getting ready to close, and we all leave before it does. It's just a safety precaution." Looking at him, I knew he was lying. Although I hadn't done anything wrong, I was afraid to go home.

As if shit couldn't get any worse when I made it home, Herc wasn't there. As a matter of fact, he didn't even come home. I spent the rest of my birthday night drunk and crying my eyes out. The shit hurt so bad. Back when I first got pregnant, and we wanted to make things official, my biggest fear was running into a nigga that I had fucked before. It didn't matter that I had to do the shit to keep from getting my ass beat. The fact of the matter is the nigga still had sex with me. No one will ever understand what's it's like to always feel dirty. Bumping into that nasty ass bitch had me feeling filthy. Herc was so embarrassed and ashamed he couldn't even look at me. If he said that he wasn't, he would be lying. His reaction showed and proved that a man of his caliber just couldn't accept my past. It doesn't matter that he's seen the real Princess Delgado. It doesn't matter that I've given birth to his son, or that I sleep with him every night. Hell, it doesn't even matter that we're supposed to get married. I'll still be considered a whore in his and everyone else's eyes.

THE NEXT MORNING I woke up sick as a dog and unable to keep anything down. The hangover I had was one from the depths of hell. I was thanking my lucky stars my mother came and got the kids from Delilah to keep for the weekend.

As I vomited for what felt like the thousandth time, I cried. Hercules never came home, and he hadn't called. I wasn't worried that something had happened to him. If something had happened to him, this place would be filled with family. I tried calling him, and he didn't answer. My ass was sick, sad, and hurt. For some reason, I felt like I knew where Herc was. I just prayed my woman's intuition was wrong.

After gathering myself, I drove to the city and parked outside of A'more's house. I knew where she lived because one day I followed Herc after finding out who she was at Gustavo's coming home party. I knew Herc was fucking her. Women don't behave like she was doing unless she was getting the dick.

I wiped the tears that had fallen down my face. The tears were falling at such a rapid succession that I could barely see. However, I could see Herc's Maserati parked out front. Most women would have got out and knocked on the door for their man. Hell, many would have destroyed the car, but I couldn't bring myself to even get out of the car. It was like I was numb and my legs were like lead and couldn't move.

After a while, I ended up back at the house. How I made it home without crashing was a miracle. Before heading up the stairs, I grabbed a bottle of Tito's from the bar and headed up the stairs. Looking in the medicine cabinet, I grabbed the Percocet's that I had been secretly taking just to ease some of the stress I was under. Climbing into bed, I opened the pill bottle and took as many as I could swallow. Opening the Tito's, I drank it straight washing all of the pills down. I honestly wasn't trying to kill myself. All I wanted was to sleep this shit away. I needed to be numb so that my heart could no longer hurt. As much as I loved my life and my kids, my soul was growing weary. I just didn't want to feel any more pain. I just wanted to wake up and feel okay.

TEN

QUEENIE

I had smoked damn near a whole pack of Newports while waiting on a word about Princess. I'm having a hard time understanding how I left her smiling last night, and this morning I found her unresponsive. I didn't want to believe that she had been through so much that she decided to kill herself. The pill and liquor bottle that laid next to her were true signs that she actually tried to kill herself. However, I prayed that this shit was an accident.

After hours of me crying, I had finally gathered myself. I asked God to spare my daughter and take my worthless ass. Her life was more important than mine was. Princess needed to wake up so that she could get home to her kids. Hercules was currently on a rampage and feeling like Princess didn't give a fuck about him or the kids.

My heart hurt watching him cry because I do know that he loves Princess. He just needs to learn how to handle things better. Hearing him talking about taking the kids from her wasn't cool. He needed to at least wait until she wakes up to see what was going on with her. Everyone had been in the hospital waiting for word on Princess, but Hercules sent everybody home except Diego and Miami. I'm glad Passion had Gustavo sitting by her side because she was a wreck. Just observing how she was carrying on showed just how much she cared about Princess.

"I can't believe this. Princess would never try to hurt herself. She's too happy and excited about the wedding, not to mention studying so hard for her GED. A person who is making future plans doesn't just wake up one day and decide to kill their self. Something happened. When we left her last night, she was happy. What happened Herc?" Miami shed tears as she spoke. I know that she really cares for my daughter, and I love her for that.

"I don't know what the fuck happened!"

"Do not yell at me, Hercules Hernandez!

"Calm down, Miami! As a matter of fact, you need to go home. This is too much on my son. Come on." Diego pulled her up from the chair, and she yanked away from him.

"Let me go I can walk on my own. This is not over, Hercules. Somebody, please call me when she wakes up."

"I promise I'll call. Just go home and rest, Miami," I assured her.

The last thing this family needed was for her to be laid up in the hospital too. Diego did not play when it came to her health. He's exactly what she needed because Miami is very hard headed. Sometimes she truly forgets that she is pregnant.

"Mr. Hernandez, you guys can come back and see Ms. Delgado. She's awake and asking for you."

I silently thanked God for waking my baby up before hauling ass to her room. Hercules damn near knocked me down getting to Princess. My heart started to beat faster than ever in anticipation of seeing my daughter. When I found her unresponsive, it scared the shit out of me.

"What are they talking about? I didn't try to kill myself, Hercules! All I did was take some Percs and drink some Tito's with it." She was uncontrollably crying as Hercules hugged her tight.

"Calm down, Princess. We know you didn't, baby. At the same time, I found an almost empty pill bottle next to you. Princess, you were unconscious. You might not have meant to kill yourself, but what you did almost killed you."

"I know, ma. It was an accidental overdose. Please tell them I'm not crazy, and nothing is wrong with me. They're trying to keep me here on a damn psych hold. Please, Hercules. You have to sign me out here."

"Princess, I can't do that. There is obviously something wrong if you even feel the need to take Percocet's in the first place. I think it is a good thing that they want you to stay for a couple of days. During that time, you can talk to someone who can help you. Although you didn't mean for this happened, you have to take into consideration that you could have died if Queenie hadn't found you in time. Then what would have happened with us? Our kids would be without a mother. I'm sorry, but I'm not going to check you out of here. As a matter of fact, when they do release you, I'm making sure to get you some professional help. I cannot be married to a woman that pops pills. I love you, but you can't be around the kids all high and shit. Apparently, you've been taking them for some time now. Lately, I've come home, and you're knocked the fuck out. I've been thinking it's because you're tired from taking care of the kids and studying all day, but all along, you've been high."

"No, Hercules! That's not true. I don't take them like that. I would never be high while I'm taking care of my kids."

"Shhh! Stop crying, Princess. Everything is going to be okay. I know you would never hurt the kids. You do need to talk to a professional though if you do need to take them to cope. I was a drug addict for many years, so I know how easy it is to get hooked."

I guess that triggered anger in Herc because he kicked over the garbage can and walked out of the room.

"I never meant for any of this to happen." Princess was beside herself at this point.

I had to make it a priority to speak with Herc about his behavior. He needs to find a better way to deal with Princess. Right now, she's in a fragile state. Instead of scolding her, he should have been more sympathetic to what was going on with her. I'm not saying pacify the fact that what she did wasn't dangerous, but he needed to also uplift her."

"I know you didn't. Don't you worry. Everything is going to be okay. I promise. Momma is going to with you every step of the way.

"I don't know what I'm going to do if he doesn't want to marry me anymore." Princess buried her face into my chest, and I cried with my daughter. It felt absolutely good to be her strength. I just wish it were under different circumstances.

As a recovering addict, the last thing I want is for my child to addicted to drugs. Them damn opiates are taken over, but the shit will not take over my child. If I have to beat it out of her, I will. In the meantime, I'm going to be the best mother that I can be to help her get through this.

MY ASS WAS STARVING, and I had to wait until Princess drifted off to sleep. It was after hours, and I knew the cafeteria was closed. It was a good thing they had vending machines with sandwiches in it. After grabbing some quick stuff to eat, I headed back up to her room. I couldn't believe Hercules had left and didn't come back. One thinks he would have at least called. This was totally not the response I expected from him. This leads me to believe that something is off with him and Princess. Hercules would never abandon Princess at a time like this. Then again, he probably couldn't handle it.

Stepping off the elevator, I bumped dead into the last person on earth that I wanted to see.

"Just the person I'm looking for. How is our daughter doing?"

"Nigga, you have lost your motherfucking mind! You must be ready to be lying downstairs in the morgue. That's exactly where your ass will be if you don't get the fuck out of my face."

Benito was blocking me from walking past him. At that moment I was pissed the fuck off for leaving my purse in Princess' room. I swear

I wanted to blow his fucking brains out and truly not give a fuck about spending the rest of my life in prison.

"You're still beautiful and feisty as ever!" He tried to stroke my face and but my reflexes made me punch his old ass in his shit. He grabbed his nose as blood started pouring out of it like a faucet.

"I advise you to get the fuck from around this hospital. Hercules is gunning for your dumb ass!"

"That's actually who I'm looking for. Here is the address to where I'm staying. Let him know he can bring all his goons if he has to. He needs to know the reason for all of this shit. I'm tired of running, and the information that I have can save not only his life but his empire as well."

"It's funny that you're standing your deceitful lying ass in front of me as if you didn't fuck me over. You betrayed me, nigga! Do you have any idea what I've been through over the years?

"I'm sorry for everything, Queenie. If I could go back in time, I would change everything. You might not believe me, but hurting you is my biggest regret."

The nigga standing before me was absolutely disgusting and a liar. He lies faster than a cat can lick its own ass, and I don't believe shit coming out of his mouth.

"You're so full of shit Benito, or should I call you Juan. Whoever the fuck you are today, I deserve an explanation for the lies. At the same time, I don't even want it. I do have one question for you though? Why would you kidnap our daughter and take her to Medellin? You don't have to like me Benito, but I thought someone murdered her at first. Princess has been through so much, and she didn't deserve that."

"You're right. She didn't deserve that. At the time, I was so caught up in this shit with Humberto that it was hard to get out. He was threatening to kill Princess, so I decided to pay Hector to take her. I was never trying to hurt or kill her in any way. I was protecting her from an unseen force that she had no clue about. Her life is still in danger because Humberto has a hit out on his own son. The kids aren't even safe, so it's imperative he comes to see me sooner or later."

I snatched the card away from him because I was still pissed off at him and I would forever be pissed off at him.

"It's funny that you were free all of those years living your best fucking life while we suffered. Princess has needed you all of her life. You're a pitiful ass excuse of a man and a coward. The only reason you're here portraying yourself to be the caring father is because Humberto is on your ass. I'll give Hercules the card, but you stay the fuck away from Princess and Passion. Those girls don't need shit from your deceitful ass." I pushed his ass out of my way with so much force that he almost fell.

When I made it back to Princess' room, she was still sleeping soundly. Grabbing my phone, I quickly sent a text to Hercules. Shit was definitely about to hit the fan.

ELEVEN

HERCULES

Livid wasn't the word for the way I was feeling. Just knowing that the nigga Benito had got that close to Princess had me pissed the fuck off. I'm just glad Queenie called me immediately. Without hesitation, I checked Princess out of the hospital. Although in my heart I knew she needed to stay on the psych hold for the seventy hours, at the same time, she would be safer at home. This time around, Queenie would be sitting with her around the clock while I was out trying to get at this nigga Benito. He must have really wanted to die popping up like shit is sweet.

"Queenie, are you sure he said he wanted to discuss some shit about Humberto?"

"Yes, Herc. He made it clear that Humberto is behind all of this. He looked pitiful if you ask me. That nigga Humberto has got to be on his ass. That's the only thing I can think of that would make him want to talk to you knowing you want to murder his dumb ass." I stared at the card with his address on it, and all I could see was red. I finally had a location on this motherfucker, and now I have to tread lightly because he has vital information that I need. Just when I wanted to torture and kill his bitch ass, I needed to hold off in an effort to get to my father.

"I'm going to go meet up with his bitch ass. Don't tell Princess anything about this. I don't need her under any more stress than she already is."

"Don't worry. I have everything under control here. You should at least go and talk to her. I want to say more, but I don't want to overstep my boundaries. I've just built a relationship with her, and you've finally accepted me into your family. I love you guys, but you have to do better with communication. Besides that, make sure you kick Benito's ass real good for me."

Hearing the baby cry Queenie rushed to get him out of the swing. The lil nigga was getting fat as hell. He looked like he barely could breathe. I definitely needed to go to one of his appointments with Princess. Before heading out to see what's to this nigga Benito, I went to check on Princess. She had been home a couple of hours, and we hadn't said a word to one another. I wasn't mad at her. However, I was disappointed and shocked. A nigga truly didn't know she even owned Percocet. The whole thing was making me feel like I had been so consumed with murdering motherfuckers that I wasn't paying attention to my future wife. I should have known that she was stressing. Walking inside the room, I observed Princess sitting up in bed watching TV.

"You good. I was about to head out to handle some business and wanted to see if you need anything?"

"Nah. I'm straight," she said with an attitude as she waved me off. That's when I noticed that she wasn't wearing her engagement ring.

"Where the fuck your ring at?"

"It's over there on the nightstand."

"Why the fuck is it over on there on the nightstand and not on your fucking finger?"

"The engagement is off, Hercules." She was speaking so nonchalant, and I was ready to go ballistic.

"I understand you're not in a good space mentally, but your ass is not crazy, Princess. I'm about to head out to handle some business, and when I come back, you better have your fucking ring on! Stop fucking playing with me, Princess. My patience is running real fucking thin with you."

"Well, let your patience run the fuck out and send my hoe ass on my way. I'm sure the bitch A'more will be right there waiting for you."

"What the fuck does she have to do with anything?"

"She has everything to do with it. I saw your car parked in that bitch's driveway the night you didn't come home. Don't stand there looking all shocked and stupid. How could you just leave me at my own birthday party like that? Were you that embarrassed hearing that nigga talk like that? I can assure you that you were not more embarrassed than me. You have no clue what it's like to be talked about like that in front of the person you're getting ready to marry. Your behavior showed me that you couldn't handle my past, and I'm tired of apologizing for shit that was out of my control. I'm not the same girl that Lucifer had doing all types of shit. I went and had that tattoo removed and everything trying to prove to you, I'm not that girl. I don't cheat or anything. But, the moment I piss you off, you run to that bitch's house. I've told your ass I'm not Bleu, and you will not carry me that way. I'll go back to co-parenting if it means keeping my dignity and self-respect as a woman.

You can't stand in front me and say you accept me and when my past is thrown in my face, you reject me. By the way, I didn't try to kill myself. However, seeing your car parked in that bitch's driveway when you didn't come home hurt my soul. The last thing I want to do is kill myself and leave my kids motherless. I just wanted to numb the pain of my life. I'm tired of hurting, Hercules! Go head on and take care of whatever business you have to take care of. Just leave me alone."

At that moment, I wanted to tell her the reason for me being over there, but I couldn't. I would have to take her being mad at me for right now. I was on my way to handle some shit that required all of my attention. Walking over to the nightstand, I grabbed the ring and walked over to where she was in bed. I damn near broke her finger trying to put the ring back on.

"Don't take that fucking ring off your finger again! As soon as I handle this shit out here in these streets, I'll be back to discuss this."

A nigga did feel like shit for walking out of her birthday party because she didn't deserve that. At the same time, that was the first time that I had inquired another nigga that she fucked. I had put it in my head that I was the only nigga that had graced her walls. Having the nigga up front and in my face shined the harsh reality of what Princess had been through. It wasn't even about being reminded of her past that had me in my feelings. It was more so this nigga was literally lusting over her. I had to leave before I murked his ass in front of a club full of people. That's how my car ended up at A'more's house. I grabbed her car, came back to the club, and caught the nigga snoozing and trunked his ass. Let's just say his blatant disrespect is going to have his people on the news pleading for his whereabouts. I move a certain type of way for a reason. I've never actually put in work in front of Princess, and I want to keep it that way. The less she knows, the better off she'll be. Obviously, she's not ready for that part of me. Honestly, I never want her to be. Princess isn't that typical ride or die who stands beside her nigga shooting guns and shit. I'm the type of that nigga that doesn't even want her to do shit like that. Her job is to be a beautiful wife and a loving mother. My job is to protect her, and that's why I'm eliminating all threats one by one. Princess is going to get her happily ever after by any means necessary.

"YOU HAVE five minutes to let me know why the fuck you crossed me and inflicted pain on my family!"

I was holding a gun to the back of Benito's head. For hours, I sat outside and waited for him to grab the morning paper. Why the fuck he wants to know what's going in the world is beyond me, especially since he's a dead man.

"I've been expecting you. I'm surprised you came alone."

"This shit is personal. Now you have four minutes to tell me why the fuck you've been working with my father." This nigga was running the fuck out of time. My trigger finger was itching, and it wouldn't be long before I put a round in his shit.

"You can put your gun away. I'm here alone, and I can assure you I'm not a threat to you. I never wanted you dead at all. That was Hector acting on Humberto's command. All I've ever wanted was to keep the drugs moving so that my money could keep flowing. I only kidnapped my daughter because her life was and still is in danger. You see Humberto wants you and your bloodline dead. Your sons are especially in grave danger. They are your successors, and he wants them killed on sight. I don't know what you did to him, but he is out for blood. The only reason I'm still alive is because he wants me to do it. When you came to Medellin to rescue Princess and Sophia, I was here. Humberto wanted me to murder my own grandson, and that would never happen. It didn't matter if it meant my life being on the line. I would gladly die to save the lives of my daughter and grandson. As a matter of fact, I would never kill a child. I'm a cold-hearted nigga, but kids and woman are off limits. No matter what's going on, I need Princess to understand that it was never my intention to hurt her. Truthfully speaking, I've failed her all of her life. I've failed Passion as well. I'm glad all of this happened because it has brought my daughters together. I would like for you to give each of them one of these envelopes. There is one there for Queenie too. She has hurt the most out of all of this."

With my gun still trained on him, he walked over to the bar poured himself two shots and handed me the envelopes.

"Where can I find Humberto?"

"He's in Las Vegas with a residency at the MGM."

"Are my uncles aware that he's back?"

"He murdered them. That's why you never knew who was actually behind it all. Please tell my daughters that I'm sorry for every-thing that I did to them, and I hope one day they can find it in their hearts to forgive me."

With those being his final words, I sent a bullet through his skull. There was no need for him anymore. He allowed greed to cloud his judgment. I didn't care about how he got out of prison. The shit had nothing to do with me. My only concern was him telling me where the fuck Humberto was. Benito was a liar. He didn't give a fuck about anybody but himself. Had I not gone to Medellin and dismantled his empire there, he would never have spared my son. After setting the house ablaze, I headed to make shit right with Princess. If she had that fucking ring off, I was going to murder her ass next. Everybody was stressing me the fuck out. I couldn't wait to get home and smoke a fat ass blunt.

ABOUT AN HOUR LATER, I was walking into the house. The sounds of Baby Herc screaming and crying at the top of his lungs alerted me. I found him and Princess in the kitchen. She was walking back and forth trying to soothe him.

"What's wrong with him Princess?"

"He's teething, and he has an earache. I already called his doctor, and he told me just to give him some Tylenol. He's hungry now, so once I feed him, he should calm down. My momma and Queenie have been holding him while he's sleeping, so now he expects me to do it, and that is not about to happen."

"What's up, lil nigga? You don't feel good?" I kissed him on the forehead, and he laid his head on my shoulder. He immediately stopped crying. The look on Princess' face was priceless. She couldn't believe he had instantly stopped crying.

"Don't laugh, ain't shit funny. He has been fussy for hours. Here, I'm going to go upstairs and lie down. I have a migraine out of this world."

Princess handed me the bottle, and I tried to kiss her. She blocked my shit and walked away. I shook my head because I knew her ass was on that stubborn shit once again. As I fed and rocked my son to sleep, I figured out a way to make shit right with Princess. I just hoped she allowed me to make everything right.

Baby Herc finally went to sleep. Since he was a little warm, I decided to let him sleep in the room with us instead of his own. Princess would like that since she made it a habit to sneak him in the bed with us every night anyway.

"We're going to have to cut back on his damn milk intake. This nigga heavy as shit."

"That's more than just milk. Queenie and Delilah are feeding him mashed potatoes, and God knows what else."

I handed the baby to her and headed to the bathroom to take a shower. As I let the water run all over me, I couldn't help but think about what was in the envelopes Benito gave me. At first, I was going to throw the bitches out, but then again he might be giving them the closure they all need. I would give them all to Princess. She would be in control of giving the letters to Passion and Queenie. I wanted no parts of that. It was bad enough he gave me the shit to begin with. The whole encounter was off to me. As bad as I wanted to kill him when all the shit first kicked off, it all subsided when I finally got the motherfucker in front of me. Once I found out my father was behind it all, I got tunnel vision.

All I want is to kill his ass. At the same time, this shit hurt and not being able to talk about it is killing me. On the one hand, I want to be open and honest with Princess. On the other hand, I don't think she'll be able to handle any more bullshit. Despite her going through hell being with Lucifer I hated that she had to come with me and go through shit as well. Life with me is supposed to be different. After everything we've been through this year, we're due for some good shit to happen to us.

After showering, I dried off and joined Princess in bed. I smiled noticing that she still had her ring on. She was lying in bed staring at the ceiling in deep thought. I knew shit was weighing heavy on her, so I needed to just do something to ease her troubled spirit. As I placed our son in the baby bed, I climbed in bed next to her. Her stubborn ass turned over with the quickness. Princess was definitely about to make this shit hard for a nigga.

"I just want you to know that I didn't fuck A'more. I didn't come home that night because I was handling some business."

"It doesn't matter Hercules. You made it perfectly clear when we got together commitment wasn't your thing. It's my fault for thinking that I was enough. As far as business goes, I know that it comes before me anyway. I'm good, Herc. You don't owe me anything."

"Man, cut the bullshit! The business I was handing was killing that bitch ass nigga that disrespected you. I parked my car at A'more house and used one of her cars. I can assure you that I don't fuck with that bitch like that anymore. I apologize for walking out on you that night. That shit was wrong and disrespectful on my part. You didn't deserve that. Hearing that nigga speak like that did something to me. I wanted to murder that motherfucker right there. The old me would have, but I couldn't do that shit in front of you. Maybe I should have. My reckless ass behavior caused you to hurt and overindulge to the point where you could have killed yourself." Princess quickly turned over in bed and sat up.

"I swear to you Hercules I wasn't trying to kill myself. I'll admit I was in my feelings and it caused me to drink and take the Percocet. It's not something that I do all the time. Just in case you're wondering, I no longer have the desire to even take Percocet's simply to cope. I'm sorry for even doing that shit and being reckless. The last thing I want to do is leave the kids without their mother."

"What about me, Princess? You want to leave a nigga?"

"Absolutely not. I never want to leave you. It's just that I can't deal with you loving me one day, and then you shun me when my past is brought up. I can't live like that. I want to be with you the rest of my life, but I'm tired of apologizing for things that were out of my control. That's why I took off the ring? Maybe you're not really ready for marriage. We can be a couple and not be married.

"You talking stupid as fuck right now! Call everybody right now and tell them to pack for Vegas. I'm more than ready to make you my wife. Fuck waiting months and putting together a big wedding. Let's do this ASAP!"

"Are you serious right now?"

"I'm serious as fuck. We're going to Vegas and get married. I can't wait to make you my wife, and I mean that shit. Let me make a couple of calls to my people out there. "

Going to Vegas would kill two birds with one stone. I can get married and kill my father at the same time. The shit will work out perfectly.

"Herc, I've already spent money to hold the venue. It wasn't cheap either. We will lose the money."

"Fuck that money! I'm ready to marry you and show you that you mean more to me than anything in this world. Plus, you might get the urge to take the ring off again. I need to hurry up and give your stubborn ass my last name."

"I'm ready to rock your last name as well."

I kissed Princess passionately and headed to my office. I needed to holla at some of my people to get some shit in place for Vegas. Even though it was some last minute shit, I still wanted the shit to be right for Princess. She deserved something nice. I saw how hard she had been going with the wedding plans, so a nigga definitely needed to make the shit special even if it was last minute.

TWELVE

PRINCESS

Excited wasn't the word for the way I was feeling. Just hearing Hercules say let's get married now shifted my whole mood. Taking those pills and drinking that damn liquor put so much into perspective. I needed to find a different way to cope. Lord knows I didn't try to kill myself, but I'm positive the whole family thinks I did. They've been tiptoeing around me like I'm a damn recovering crack head or something. I'm glad we're going to Vegas to get married. It might be exactly what we need to get to our happy place. Lord, knows we deserve it. We've taken so many losses that we're due for a win.

Since Hercules had gone to his office to make some phone calls, I decided to shower and put on something sexy. I was in need for some of that daddy dick. Taking notice of some envelopes on the dresser, I picked them up. Noticing there were three envelopes with Queenie, Passion, and my name on it, I became curious. I didn't open the ones that were addressed to them, but I did open mine.

Tearing it open, my eyes bulged out of my head looking at a ten million dollar check from Benito. I had to take a seat on the edge of the bed to gather myself.

"I see that you found the letters."

Briefly looking up at Hercules, I took notice of his facial expression. It was then I realized that he had placed them there. Having them in his possession meant he'd finally caught up with Benito.

"Is he dead?"

"Yes, he's dead. What was in the envelope?"

"A check for ten million dollars. I'm assuming there is a check here for Queenie and Passion."

"Yes, he wanted me to give them to you guys, but I think you should do it. Our flight leaves Saturday, so you have tomorrow to give it to them. Come on. Let's get some rest. It's been a long week, my love."

Hercules walked over to where I was on the bed and removed the envelopes from my hand. As he cut off the lights and casually laid down, I wanted to ask how he caught Benito. Then again, the less I knew, the better. It wasn't like I gave a fuck anyway. He was no good to me alive, but he damn sure did me a little good in death. Hearing Hercules lightly snoring, I guess could cancel wanting some damn dick. It was obvious he was tired. Just looking at his handsome face while he slept I knew that he was stressed out. At least Benito was one less thing he had to worry about. At the same time, I couldn't help but feel like there was more going on than he was saying. I hated that Herc felt like he couldn't tell me anything. Then again, almost overdosing didn't help me at all. He definitely thinks I'm fragile as fuck now. Whatever it is that's going on that I don't know about, he needs to handle it. All I want is to move forward and be a happy family. Our kids deserve it.

I couldn't sleep, so I decided just to go ahead and take the GED test. It had been available online for me to take it. As I started, I was nervous as hell, but I took my time. I had been studying so hard that the answers were coming to me like second nature. Once I was finished taking it, I was sure that I passed with flying covers.

As my eyes finally got heavy, I spoke life into Hercules and our household. I've never really had a relationship with God, but he seemed to always show up when I needed him most and sometimes unexpectedly. I just needed him to cover us and keep us strong. The devil is busy, and we've been letting him win all this time. One thing for sure and two for certain, the devil no longer had power over this family. Going to Vegas and getting married was just what we needed. I just had to get pass giving these checks to my mother and sister. Queenie about to talk so much shit that it won't be funny.

"I KNOW y'all are wondering are why I invited y'all out to eat on such short notice. It was important that I had a sit down with both of you."

Queenie, Passion, and I were sitting at Outback eating having drinks. Since our food hadn't come yet, and the liquor was flowing, I decided that this was the perfect time to give them their envelopes.

"Girl, you got me nervous as hell. I hope you not about to tell us you're dying or no shit like that. We just got found each other, and I can't lose your ass already. My blood pressure is still up from that stunt you pulled last week."

I fell out listening to Passion talk. She hadn't been in Chicago that long and she was something else. Being around Queenie and Marisol was definitely rubbing off on her.

"Your ass is crazy. I'm not about to die no time too soon.

"Well, what the hell did you call us out here for?" Queenie was so damn impatient. I took the envelopes out and handed them each one.

"Open them." I took a drink from my Patrón Margarita and waited for their response.

"How did you get this?" Passion asked.

"He gave them to Hercules. Don't ask me the details because I don't know."

"He thinks giving me fifty million dollars will make up for the hell he put me through? Well, that motherfucker was right! All is forgiven but not forgotten. Let's go to the bank and make sure this nigga didn't write us a bad check. The bitch is not reliable or dependable."

"They're real. I was able to deposit mine before I met up with you. There was no way I was about to give y'all bad checks and have to her your mouth, ma!" I was thinking the same way Queenie was thinking at the moment. I made sure to go to the bank and check. Benito was definitely not to be trusted.

"How are you feeling, Passion? Even though he hurt all of us. He actually raised you, so I know you feel some type away."

"I'm not going to lie and say it doesn't make me sad because it does. However, I'll gladly accept this ten million for my pain and suffering. At the same time, we all deserved better. He should have been a man and apologized the right way. Him writing checks just prove that he's indeed a coward.

This motherfucker!" Passion stood up, and I looked behind me to see what had her attention. It was Gustavo and a female walking with two girls. I was almost positive that it was his baby momma Gia I had heard about. I was unaware if he and Passion ever had a conversation about her, so I stayed in my lane and didn't speak on it.

"You want to beat them up?" I asked, and I was serious as hell because I told his big ass not to play with my sister if he wasn't going to keep it real with her.

"Hell nah! Both of y'all sit the fuck down. Passion, you have to play this gangsta. There is no need to confront his dumb ass in a public place especially while they got kids with them. Wait until later. Ask his ass where he been at and if he lies, then you buss his shit. I swear I never want another nigga. I'll continue letting my rabbit get me off. These niggas lie faster than a cat can lick its own ass."

"I knew I should never have given that nigga my virginity last night! Now I'm sitting here with a sore ass pussy, and he is walking around like he a happy family man. Get me the fuck out of here before I be going to jail. The last thing I want to do is go to jail behind murdering a family because they all getting it. I'm sorry, but I'm not sorry. Gustavo had no business fucking me the way he did."

I was trying my best not to laugh because Passion was so serious at the moment. We hurried up and rushed out of the restaurant. Once we made it outside, Passion walked fast towards the parking lot. She was walking around looking for his car.

"Here, girl get this damn ice pick." That's gone put a big hole in it." I laughed my ass off watching Queenie hand her tools to fuck this man car up.

"Would y'all come on before we get caught?"

My ass was nervous because I just knew some of their security saw us doing damage to this man Benz. The last thing I need is to be in jail, and Hercules has to come bond me out behind Passion's bullshit.

"I'm going to go ahead and go to the bank. I'll see y'all in the morning at the airport."

"Okay, ma. I love you." Both Queenie and I stopped in our tracks as I spoke the words. I was even more surprised with myself just saying the words. I literally don't remember ever saying to her.

"I love you too, Princess. More than you will ever know." She blew me a kiss and hopped in her car.

Finally, having a healthy relationship with my mother means everything to me. There were days when I vowed to kill her if I ever saw her again. It took me to go through so much to realize that everybody needs their mother no matter what. That's why I'm extremely grateful for Hercules being diligent with bringing us back together. Had it not been for him, I don't think I ever would have talked to Queenie again in my life. Behind that gangsta ass demeanor he rocks, Herc has a heart that is as pure as gold.

Once Queenie drove away, Passion and I hopped in my car and left the parking lot. The whole time she sat in the passenger seat quietly. I could tell that she was hurt but didn't really want to talk about the bullshit, which was understandable.

"Are you okay, sis?"

"Yeah, I'm straight. That nigga has been telling me how he and his baby momma don't see eye to eye. They looked mighty cool to me. I think I'm madder because he lied about where he was at. Not even thirty minutes before he walked his ass in there, I texted him. This nigga said he was helping Herc handle some shit and he would get back at me as soon as he finished. I know he has to have contact with her because they share kids. At the same time, if he has to lie about spending time with his kids, then we have a big problem."

"I agree he shouldn't have lied. Make sure you address that shit now. That way later on down the road, it won't be any more bullshit. Now I've been through my fair share of things with Herc that made me question him. Recently, I jumped to conclusions, and it almost cost me my husband, my kids, and most importantly my life. Just give him a chance to explain before you go across his shit like Queenie told you to do."

"Why the fuck you didn't give that motivational ass speech before I put holes in the man tires?"

"I'm sorry, sis. That motivational shit just comes to me on a whim. I love your crazy ass, sis."

"I love you too. Are you ready to be Mrs. Hercules Hernandez? If your ass not I am. We're about to have so much fun at your bachelorette party. "

"I'm definitely ready to have a blast and rock that nigga's last name. Keep that bachelorette party on the low. If Herc gets wind of that shit, he's going to shut it down."

"Yeah, you right. Speaking of Vegas, run me by the bank so I can deposit this check. I've got to get home and get packed so that I can be ready in the morning. Hercules said he is leaving anybody who not ready. That man is ready to tie the knot, sis."

"Yes, he is. I just hope we get the happily ever after we deserve.

"Don't worry. Y'all are good people, and God is going to give you everything you deserve."

It felt good hearing Passion speak life into us. I appreciated that because some people would rather kill your spirit in regards to your nigga instead of lifting you. She's seen some bad since coming here with us, and she's seen some good. I'm just happy she's not letting the bad outweigh the good, which would make her pass judgment on our relationship. All my life I wanted a sibling. I hate to say this, but I'm happy Benito kidnapped me. I would never have met my sister, and I'm just happy we have each other. We're probably the best thing Benito ever created.

THIRTEEN

PASSION

All day I had been trying my best not to think about the fact that Gustavo lied to me. It was beyond me why he even felt like he had to. I do regret poking holes in his tires before addressing the situation. At the same time, he didn't have to lie in the first place. His bullshit added with my father giving me a damn check was all too much.

In my heart, I knew he was dead. Hercules is not the type of man that allows some shit to slide. After what he did to Princess, I'm almost positive that Hercules killed him. I'm not sad because he's dead. I'm sadder because he wasted so many years being a snake that he never gave our father-daughter relationship a chance. It's crazy how I simply came to a city where I knew no one, yet Princess and her family welcomed me with open arms. I've never been loved this way in all of my life. Hercules was the hardest to persuade, but even he has come around. I'm just grateful to be a part of this family. The way they go hard for one another is amazing to me, especially Hercules and Princess. They're the definition of a bipolar ass couple. One minute they're at each other's throats, and the next they're down each other's throat. Through it all, they never miss a beat when it comes to taking care of their kids. I could only hope to have my own little family and build something great.

Since I was fully packed and ready to take flight in the morning, I decided to take a hot bath and drink me some wine. Some relaxation was well needed after the long day I've had. I think I was more stressed behind Gustavo still not reaching out to me since our text earlier. He had to know that I was the one who poked the holes in his tires. If his ass knows, he could at least call and speak on the shit, instead of having me going crazy trying to figure out if he knows or not.

Just the thought of Gustavo sends chills up my spine. That man is fine as fuck. He looks just like the dude Rio that plays on the TV show, *Good Girls*. Prison did his body damn good because he was cut the fuck up. His chest and arms were so big that he looked like he lifted refrigerators for a living. When Gustavo came at me, I wasn't sure of his motives. What would an experienced man like him want with a virgin like me? Outside of the fact that he would be the first to ever get this pussy.

For two months, we spent time together. He took me out on dates and showed me all around Chicago. I fell in love with him when he took me to dinner on the top floor of the John Hancock building. It was like nothing I had ever seen. All of the tall buildings in downtown was all new to me. Medellin didn't have things like that. I was thanking my lucky stars that my parents talked to me mainly in English. That was one of the things they did right. My experience here has been much better than expected because I can speak English.

Gustavo has found it hard to believe that I've never been here before. I may have never been to Chicago, but I know now that I'm right where I'm supposed to be. Whatever this thing is that Gustavo and I are doing, I pray it works out. This shit will be devastating if I gave him my virginity, and he turns out to be some hoe ass nigga. I swear I will lose my shit if he does. Besides his indiscretion today, he has been the best man ever to me.

"SO YOU'RE JUST GOING to flatten my tires and not say shit to me?"

I looked at Gustavo like he had lost his mind. We were now on the airplane getting ready to head to Vegas, and this nigga was talking to me like this shit didn't happen yesterday. I haven't heard or talked to him since our last text.

"All of this space on this private plane and you choose to sit next to me. As far as your tires go, I don't have a clue what you are talking about." He laughed, and I didn't find shit funny.

"Really Passion? I had the manager at the restaurant run the tapes back. I saw your ass, not to mention Queenie crazy ass handing you some shit to poke my tires." He had me right there, but I didn't give a fuck.

"If you knew I poked holes in your tires, why are you just not saying something?" I wouldn't even look at him. I just continued to scroll through my phone.

"The reason I didn't say anything because I knew you were in your feelings about seeing me with my baby momma and our daughters."

"Let's get some shit straight. I wasn't in my feelings because you were with them. I had an issue with you lying. You had no reason to lie to me about spending time with your daughters. The only reason you would lie is if you were spending time with your baby momma. She was before my time, and I understand. Just let me know what the fuck it is and what the fuck it ain't so that a bitch can move expeditiously, my nigga."

Gustavo had me all the way fucked up talking about I was in my feelings.

"You ain't going nowhere, and neither am I. Let's get some shit straight. My baby momma and I are over. Yesterday we met up to discuss child support and visitation. The bitch is known for wilding, but she is pregnant by another nigga and over me, which I'm happy about because the last thing I need is her trying to come in between you and me, not to mention keeping my babies Gabby and Maddy away from me. I've been away from them all of their lives, and I don't want to miss a beat. I'm sorry for lying to you. I should have kept it real and told you. Hell, I should have brought you to meet them. Trust and believe my baby momma is the last bitch on this earth that I want anything to do with. I'm trying to build a future with you."

"Oh really?" I heard his ass talking, but I wasn't moved with the latter part of his explanation. I did, however, understand his reasons in regards to his daughters. I didn't have to let him know that though.

"Hell yeah, Passion. I'm so serious. I fucked up one time and you ready to stop fucking with me. Damn! Don't I at least deserve a second chance to make shit right with you?"

"Don't do my mine like that, sis? You got him on this motherfucker begging like Keith Sweat."

"Shut up Diego and mind your business! You were just begging too." Miami said and had the whole plane laughing.

"I say don't give in easy!"

"Stay out of this shit, Queenie. You're the reason why my shit is in the shop now. I saw your ass hand her that damn ice pick to fuck up my shit. You lucky Princess is my girl or else I would give your ass a leg shot. Why the fuck are you carrying around a damn ice pick anyway?"

"Yeah aight! Nigga, you shoot me you won't shoot nobody else. I keep my ice pick on me in case somebody jumps stupid. They won't know what the fuck hit they ass. Before they know it, they on the ground with holes all in their ass."

We all laughed at Queenie because she was dead ass serious.

"Stop playing with my sister, Gustavo! You almost caught a beat down yesterday."

"While all y'all ganging up on my boy like that. Let him make shit right with his lady. Princess, come here let me make you a part of the mile high club?"

"What's that?" Princess was so damn green. Even I knew what the mile high club was.

"Follow me." Hercules winked his eye at her, and they headed towards the bathroom. We all started clapping and making whistling sounds as they headed towards the bathroom.

"Now back to us. Do you forgive a nigga?" Gustavo lifted my chin and kissed me passionately before staring at me for a long ass time.

"I forgive you this time, but it definitely won't be a second time. Next time I'm gone have to go across your shit for real.

"Look at you all crazy over me and shit! You only had the dick one time and you trying to kill a nigga.

"Well, it ain't my fault. Didn't nobody tell you to fuck me like that straight out the gate."

"Damn! Your ass is making my dick hard. When Herc and Princess come out that bathroom, you going to let me introduce you to the mile high club?"

"Do you even have to ask?" I was definitely down for that and whatever else.

I'm glad we made up before landing in Vegas. Lord knows I didn't want to be on vacation and in my feelings. I truly didn't know what Gustavo and I were doing, but I would go with the flow and not rush things. This relationship and sex thing were all new to me, but I planned on learning and making the best of it as I go along.

FOURTEEN

PRINCESS

It felt so good to finally be in Vegas and settled into our penthouse suite. Caesars Palace was absolutely beautiful. Hercules had gone all out because everybody that took the trip with us was in dope ass suites. My baby wasn't playing when he said we were doing it big. I'm so happy Delilah gave in and came with us. I wouldn't have it any other way. She deserved to enjoy herself too. With Hercules having business out here as well, we would be staying for a full week. That gave us a chance to spend time with the kids, party, and get ready to make this shit official.

"Ms. Princess, do you want to go out and see the sights? I'll keep the kids."

"Absolutely not! Delilah, I want you to get dressed and see the sights. You're on vacation too. I'm going to order some snacks and watch some movies with the kids. I was going to wait and give you this, but I decided to give it to you now."

I reached inside my purse and handed her ten thousand dollars cash. Her eyes lit up like a Christmas tree.

"Oh no! I can't accept this, Ms. Princess. This is too much."

"No. You go above and beyond for this family. This is from

Hercules and me. We love you so much, Delilah. Take this money and enjoy Vegas. We're staying in tonight, so get you some drinks and hit up the casino."

"Thank you so much, Ms. Princess." Delilah rushed out of the suite quick as hell.

Hercules had to go out to handle something, so I was left with the kids. With them all napping I decided to take a much-needed nap. That plane ride had me tired as hell. Just thinking of the plane ride, I knew I needed to have a sit down with Gustavo. With Passion being out here on the account of me, I wanted to ensure that she was good. I could tell that she was hurt behind him lying, but her face lit up the moment they were back on good terms. Lord, I know the feeling. That's exactly how Hercules makes me feel. Lying down, I silently prayed that this vacation went off without any damn issues.

"WAKE UP, BABE!" Hearing Hercules calling my name I quickly set up. It was now dark as hell outside. My ass had slept the whole day away.

"Oh shit! I slept longer than I intended to. Where are the kids? I wanted to have a movie night with them.

"They're in the sitting area with their pajamas on watching *Boss Baby*. Ziyon is not happy about that, but you know that's Sophie's favorite movie. They've already eaten, and they have snacks for their movies. Bonnie and Clyde are even sitting down and watching TV."

"You gave them baths and fed them?" I had to ask because Hercules isn't the typical hands-on father.

"Why you ask like that? I'm not that fucked up as a father, am I?"

"No baby! You're a great father. It's just that I'm used to being the one that feeds and bathes them. By the time you come home, we're all in bed. I am happy you did it though."

"I came in here, and you were sleeping so good that I decided not to bother you and do it for a change. Are you ready for your dress fitting tomorrow?"

"Yeah, I just pray that I don't have a hard time finding what I like. I want something that lights up the room and slim fitting. I don't want all that extra over the top shit. I'm going for simple and beautiful."

"You're already simple and beautiful. I say go over the top and steal the show."

"Just me being in the room is going to steal the show."

"I hear that shit. The fellas and I are going to get fitted in the morning as well. That's another reason why we're all laying low tonight. The last thing we need is to get fucked up and miss the appointment. I do not want to hear your mouth." I laughed because he knew me well.

Before we decided to just come out to Vegas to get married, he'd missed all of our bridal appointments. Now that I'm thinking about it, it's a good thing he did want to come out here and get married. It's less stress on both of us, and I can depend on him to be on time and show up for appointments."

"I'm so happy that we've come out here to make things official. I can't wait to become Mrs. Hercules Hernandez." I waved my massive rock at his ass. All he could do is smile. He prided himself on me wearing that big ass ring. He thinks I be taking it off being petty and stubborn all the time, but it's heavy as hell.

"Hell, I can't wait either. This wedding shit is more stressful than I could have imagined. I'm sorry for not fully participating when you were trying to put it together. I'm just glad my people out here got everything in place for us. All we have to do is handle our shit and show the fuck up."

Just listening to Hercules talk about the wedding let me know he was really to take our shit to the next level. At that moment all of my worries and fears went away. It was just a couple of days before the wedding, and it wasn't getting here fast enough.

After showering and putting on some pajamas, I joined Herc and the kids. We watched movies and loved on each other. I used to dream of days like this. I spoke having a husband and kids that loved me into my life, and it manifested. No matter the bad shit that has gone on in my life, I thank God that it happened because it got me where I am today. Lucifer thought he no one would want me in this life but what he didn't know was that he was setting me up for the best man a bitch could ever ask for. Hercules Hernandez is everything, and I'm about to spend the rest of my life with him.

"OH MY GOD! You look beautiful, Princess!" Queenie said with tears in her eyes.

My mother, Miami, Passion, and Marisol were all here at the bridal shop with me. This was like the twentieth dress that I had tried on, and I think this was the one. I wish that I could FaceTime Hercules just to see if he likes it, but I know that I can't do that.

"Yes, sis, I love it too," Passion said as she situated the train of the dress.

"Bitch, if you don't say yes to the dress I want it."

"That belly is not about to stretch my damn dress out." Miami stuck her middle finger up at me, and we all laughed.

"You look amazing, Princess. I'm so happy for you. Just thinking back to us being in jail and the way you came into the family is crazy. I'm so damn happy I met you." Marisol's ass was really crying, so I had to step down off the pedestal I was on to hug her. "

I'm happy too. Who knew trafficking that white would lead me to wearing white."

"Okay now! Let's stop all of this crying and go have some drinks." Queenie jumped up from her seat as she spoke excitedly.

"Don't forget food. I can't drink, but I damn sure can eat."

"That baby keeps your ass hungry," I told Miami as I headed to the back of the store to remove the dress.

"Is this the one you want ma'am?"

"Yes, I do. I'll pay for it in full before I leave today. I would like for it to be delivered to Caesars Palace as soon as possible. I'll leave all of my guest information so that there won't be any issues."

"No need, Ms. Delgado. Your fiancé came this morning and gave me all of the instructions, and he paid for your dress in full. You have a keeper on your hands. He seems to know you like a book." The bridal consultant smiled at me and helped me out of the dress.

I was beside myself with joy. I couldn't believe Hercules had done all of that. He was playing when he said that he had everything under control. I had butterflies in my stomach just thinking about how sweet that was of him. Since he had this handled, it was time for me to start this celebration off the right way.

After drinking and eating good, we all headed back to the hotel. I was nice and litty. Hercules and all the guys were all out doing their thing most likely fucking it off at strip club or gambling. Since the rest of my girls were all tired they went to their rooms, Delilah insisted on keeping the kids in her suite with her. I decided to go downstairs to the bar and grill that was located downstairs in the hotel. My ass was on such a high that I didn't want to go to sleep until Hercules came back to the hotel.

As soon as I sat down, I noticed a familiar face but I thought my mind was playing tricks on me. That damn Tito's vodka will have a bitch seeing doubles. It was A'more sitting at the table with an old client of mine named Rico that paid big money to simply have me on his arm at events. That added with wanting to me to simply lay with him or cook dinner for him in lingerie. He used to pay Lucifer big money for me. Then he started getting obsessed and crazy. The final straw was when I caught him videotaping us having sex. Lucifer immediately cut him off, and that was about two years ago.

Just seeing him here with this bitch A'more is weird as fuck. Then my woman's intuition kicked in. This hoe was here to ruin my wedding. Had I not been tipsy, I wouldn't have even confronted her, but that liquor was a motherfucker. My silly ass should have snapped a picture and showed it to Herc but no. This bitch needed to see me, and I needed to let her ass know not to pull any bullshit because I was definitely going to kill the bitch. As far as Rico is concerned, he's nonfactor ass nigga. He better not even think of anything slick, or he would be a dead bitch too.

"What the fuck are you doing here in Vegas? Bitch, let me tell you something right now. I don't give a fuck what you and Herc had going on, but the shit is over. If you think for a minute that you're about to come here and ruin my wedding bitch, you have another thing coming."

"I'm here on business, little girl. Something you know nothing about. Head on upstairs and take care of them kids."

"Bitch, I might be younger than you, but that nigga you in love with loves me and this pussy. What you mad because he doesn't want that old cobwebbed shit you walking around with?"

"I'd rather have cobwebs instead of miles."

With that comment, I tried to jump across the table and murder her ass. I couldn't get to her, but Rico jumped in between us. I did manage to snatch her whack ass wig off of her head and launched that bitch across the bar. The hoe looked like Fire Marshall Bill by the head. She took off running in embarrassment. That's what the bitch gets. She should have thought about it before she popped slick with me.

"Okay, now ladies that's enough!"

"Get your motherfucking hands off of me!"

"Now that is no way to talk to a man that has seen you naked!"

"I don't give a fuck if you did. I'm not the Princess that you used to use for nasty, sexual perverted ass fantasies. Keep your fucking hands off of me. I don't know what type of bullshit you and that hoe are on, but it better not interfere in my wedding." This nigga had that sick ass look in his eyes, and it was pissing me off. Something wasn't right with this whole set up.

"Now why would I ever want to ruin my son's happy day."

"What did you just say?" My head immediately began to spin trying to take in what the fuck he had just said to me.

"Yeah, you heard me right. Hercules Hernandez is my son. To

him, I'm known as Humberto Hernandez. To people who don't know me, I'm Rico Rivera. I'm almost positive this whole wedding thing he's out here doing is a scapegoat to murder me. I taught him everything he knows. By the way, your father Benito proved to be the weak motherfucker he's always been. He had one job, and that was to bring you back to me. Sorry ass couldn't even do that. Tell my son I'm at the MGM Grand in the Presidential Suite. I'll be waiting for him to come see me. I want my empire back, and most importantly I want you as my queen. His money is nowhere near where mine is. Why fuck with my son when you can fuck with me?"

"I don't give a fuck how much money you got. I will never want your ass." He winked at me and walked away like he hadn't just fucked me completely up.

I was literally stuck and couldn't move. This shit wasn't happening to me right now. What are the odds of me bumping into Rico of all people? Maybe he was lying. There was no way he could be Hercules' father. Just looking at him, I knew he was telling the truth because the resemblance was uncanny. Had I not ran into him, I never would have put two and two together. What the fuck was I supposed to do now? Hercules would never marry me now knowing that I had been with his father. My head was really spinning trying to get a handle on what the fuck had just transpired. I don't understand why God is punishing me this way.

After sitting in the bar area for a little while longer, I decided to go up to the suite and wait for Hercules. I had no choice but to tell him. That is if the bitch A'more hadn't already told him. As I rode the elevator up, I couldn't help but wonder what her ulterior motive against Herc is. Was she doing this because she's a scorned woman, or was she just in cahoots with Rico like everybody else was? It's a damn shame that our own families have been trying to ruin us.

Hercules was going to go ballistic. I'm almost positive that he's going to cancel the wedding, but this is something that I can't sit back and keep a secret. I definitely can't allow the bitch A'more to tell her version first. If she knows what's good for her, she should be packing and making a run for it. Hercules was going to murder her ass on sight.

Stepping off of the elevator, I rushed trying to get into the suite. I had to sit down to catch myself because I was having a panic attack. I was so damn scared that my stomach was hurting. This shit had fucked me up. All of the liquor I had previously drunk had worn off. My ass needed a fat ass blunt and a couple of shots. Right about now, I wish that I had a damn Percocet. The shit was definitely needed for this shit that I was going through. This morning started so beautiful and was promising only to end in horribly.

After rolling a blunt, I went out on the balcony and flamed it up. I didn't have time to grab a glass. The Patrón bottle was just fine for me to drink from. Not long after, I was high as a kite and damn near drunk again. I placed my hands in the palm of my hands and started to cry. This shit was not fair. What did I do to deserve this shit that was happening to me?

"Princess! Baby, where you at?" the sound of Hercules' booming voice made me damn near jump off the balcony.

"I'm out here." I quickly wiped the tears from my face before he came out there where I was.

"What you doing out here?" He sat beside me and moved some of my hair from my face.

"We need to talk, Hercules." my voice cracked because I couldn't hold the shit in if my emotional ass wanted to.

"What's wrong, Princess?"

"Tonight I saw A'more in the grill area with this guy named Rico."

"What the fuck you mean you saw A'more? That bitch has no reason to be out here. Who the fuck is this nigga named Rico, and how the fuck do you know him?" He was now standing over me yelling, and my ass was trembling like a motherfucker.

"Please calm down!"

"Don't tell me to calm down. I come up in here, and you're crying and shit. Quit stalling and tell me what the fuck is going on!"

"Well, like I said, I went to the bar downstairs, and that's when I saw A'more sitting with Rico. Rico is a guy who used to pay Lucifer top money for me. He started acting all weird and shit, so Lucifer cut him off from me. That was the last time I ever saw him. So, when I saw him sitting with her, my antennas went up. Immediately I confronted him. She popped slick with me, so I tried to take her fucking head off. Rico called himself breaking us up. When I told him not to touch me, he started talking crazy to me. Saying he's your father and his name is really Humberto and how he knows you're here in Vegas to murder him. He told me to tell you that he's at the MGM. The thing that stuck out to me the most was that he said Benito's job was to bring me to him. What the hell is going on, Hercules? Is that really why you wanted to come here to get married?"

"We were coming to get married before I ever made the decision to murder his ass. Don't ask me no fucking questions about my personal business. The only thing you should be concerned about is how it looks that you've fucked a father and a son!" he yelled as he grabbed the Patrón bottle that I was drinking from and launched it across the room.

"I didn't know, Hercules!" I cried as I walked behind him trying to get him to stop trying to leave.

"I have to go and handle some shit, Princess. Don't bring your ass out of this room." I grabbed hold of him before he could leave out of the door.

"Are we still going to get married?" I looked and sounded so pitiful. At that moment I didn't care because he needed to let me know.

"I can't answer that right now!" He roughly yanked away from me without saying another word.

I became numb hearing his response. The tears that I was once shedding were gone. Most women would be crying, but I decided this was my life. At this point, it was time for me to stop living in this hood ass fairytale. That was some bullshit that's read in these urban fiction novels. It's obvious a happily ever after is not in the cards for me.

As I climbed up in the bed, I stared at the ceiling in deep thought. Despite Hercules finding out some news about me, it was obvious he had been hiding shit from me. It was more to coming out to get married than he tried to make it seem. He was really out here to kill Rico, or shall I say Humberto. This is the most confusing shit I've ever seen. At this point, I don't care either if we get married or if we don't. This shit is just too much to bear.

The more I laid in the bed, the angrier I became just thinking about how Hercules told me to stay my ass in the room. I was so fucking tired of this shit. Each and every time some shit pops off, I'm right in the middle of all of the bullshit. Then I'm left just sitting around and waiting for Hercules to handle shit. Not this time though. I refuse to sit around and allow my family to be destroyed.

Jumping out of bed, I rummaged throw my suitcases and found some black leggings and a black hoodie. It was a good thing I had my all black Vapormax with me. Placing the hood on my head and my gun in my hoodie pocket, I headed out of the room. For the first time in my life, I was about to stand up for myself. It was the only way that I was going to be able to stop people from fucking with me, not to mention proving to Hercules that I'm not the weak ass bitch he keeps trying to make me out to be. He's going to be mad as hell that I left the room, but I don't give a fuck at this point.

AFTER CATCHING an Uber to the MGM Grand, I braced myself as I walked inside. I didn't think about gaining access to the suite. I knew it wouldn't be easy, so I had to think fast looking around the lobby. I quickly came up with an idea as I approached the concierge. I could tell by his mannerisms that he was gay, so this would be easier than I thought.

"Hello beautiful, how can I help you?"

"As a matter of fact, you can. My father Rico Riviera is staying in the presidential suite. I lost my key card, and I was wondering if you could give me one. I would really appreciate it."

He smiled at me and started typing on the screen. My heart was racing fast as hell because I just knew his ass was probably calling security on my ass.

"Mr. Riviera has a lot of daughters that have lost their key cards this week. I'm not judging, honeyyy! Make that money baby, and don't let it make you." He winked his eyes at me and handed me the key card.

I couldn't do shit but laugh on the inside as I headed for the elevator. His old ass had all this money and still had to buy pussy. He had the nerve to compare himself to Hercules. That nigga couldn't hold a candle to my baby. He needs to stop trying to compete because there is no comparison.

Once I made it to the door, I got ready to stick the card in, but the door opened. I quickly went inside my pocket to grip my gun.

"Come in, beautiful." Rico stepped to the side and allowed me to come inside.

For some reason, I wasn't nervous. I needed to play this shit accordingly to get out of this motherfucker with my life. I stepped inside of the suite and made sure to keep my hand in my pocket gripping my gun. The anger and frustration that had built up inside of me had me ready to blow his fucking brains out if he breathed too hard.

"This is not a social call. I need to find out what the fuck is it you want with Hercules. If you're really his father, why are you trying to hurt him?"

"The Hernandez Cartel belongs to me not him. I don't know if your fiancé told you or not, but I was forced to step down. That sounded like a good decision years ago, but I no longer feel that way. I've built this empire with my blood, sweat, and tears. Watching him run it into the ground has me feeling like I need it back. Of course, I know he's not going to just hand it over to me. That's why I've been pulling out all of the stops. Imagine my surprise when I learned the one that got away was now with my son, not to mention laid up giving him babies. How are my grandkids doing anyway?" He casually sat on the sofa and flamed up a cigar like this shit was sweet.

"Don't speak on my kids. You're not their grandfather. You're not even a father to Hercules. You tried to have him killed. What type of father are you supposed to be?"

"Let's not discuss my parenting skills. Let's discuss us."

"Are you delusional, Rico?"

"Call me Humberto. My family calls me that."

"I'm not your fucking family, and there is no us. Let's be perfectly clear. I don't give a fuck what happened between us in the past. You and I will never be. This Saturday I'm marrying the man of my dreams, and you or no one else will come in between that."

He started laughing and clapping like this shit was some big ass joke.

"Look at you standing there acting all holier than thou. Just a couple of years ago, you were a human mattress. I wonder what my dear son would say if he saw the pictures and videos that I have of you. Trust me. I don't think a wedding ceremony will be taking place when he sees it. Just thinking about that pretty pink pussy has given me a hard-on. Come and sit on it one more time for old time sake."

Hearing him say that triggered something inside of me. Without hesitation, I reached for the gun inside my pocket and shot him in the chest. He was struggling and moving around too much, so I shot his ass again. I stood there in shock and damn near numb. My ass had just killed this nigga, and I was in a damn trance staring at his fat ass body.

"Princess! What the fuck are you doing here? I told you to stay inside the damn room!" Hercules' loud booming voice brought me out of the trance that I was in.

"He was trying to ruin our life." He took the gun from my hand and kissed me on the forehead. That's when I noticed he was with A'more.

"A'more is going to take you back to the hotel. I'll be there as soon as I can to explain everything. Don't ask any questions. Just listen to me. Our freedom depends on it."

I wanted to go off but I also knew now wasn't the time. He damn near pushed me out of the door. As I was going out of the room Diego, Gustavo, and Jigg were coming inside of the room.

"I know you're mad at me, but trust me nothing is going on between Herc and me. This whole time I was here in Vegas, I was trying to set Humberto up without Herc's knowledge. When you saw us earlier tonight at the bar, I was reeling him in to believe that I had a vendetta against Herc. I'm not going to lie and say I didn't feel some type of way when he cut me off. He flat out said he could no longer fuck with me on that level because he was getting ready to marry you. Hercules has been here for me through it all over the years, and that's why I fell in love with him to begin with. The love I have for him wants me to see him happy even if it's not with me. I'm sorry if I disrespected you in any way. Now let's get the fuck out of here."

I took in everything she said, and it was all cool. I must have been crazy or something because all while she was talking to me, I saw visions of her fucking my nigga.

"Thank you. I appreciate that."

I was being fake as hell with this bitch. In my heart, I know if she had the opportunity, she would try her luck with Hercules. He's not fucking with her like that. That is the only reason her ass wants to place nice. I'll play the little role with her, but I will definitely buss this hoe ass if I have to.

After the short ride back over to the hotel, I headed straight to my suite. Of course, Queenie, Miami, Passion, and Marisol were already in my suite.

"You just love running up my pressure, don't you?" my momma said.

"I did what I had to do to protect my family."

"It was dangerous and stupid as hell though."

"I know it was, Miami. That man was getting ready to ruin my family. I'm tired of people thinking they can keep holding my past over my head. Humberto really thought because I was forced to have sex with him years ago he could hold it over my head. He was sadly fucking mistaken. I'll be behind prison walls before I let another nigga think they can come around me threatening me."

I walked away from them and didn't even wait for a response. I said what I said, and I meant it. If the wedding was off, then so be it. I don't give a fuck I'm living life according to what the fuck makes Princess happy. As God is my witness, I'm no longer living off of other people's opinion me. Take me as I am, accept who I was, and love the woman that I'm becoming.

FIFTEEN

HERCULES

Standing over Princess as she slept, I didn't know if I was mad at her for defying me, or for killing Humberto before I could get to him. I needed to be the one who killed him so that I good get the closure I needed to move on with my life. At the same time, I have to commend her for standing up and being strong for our family.

I wanted to be mad, but how could I ever be mad at her. It made me feel some type of way knowing that she had actually been with my father. After promising her that her past didn't matter to me, I couldn't go back on my word. That's the whole reason for me really wanting to marry her right now. She needed to understand that her past didn't matter to me. Honestly, being with someone who wasn't perfect made me want to humble myself as a man. Here I am living like I'm the best nigga walking, but I flawed as well.

If I were perfect, I wouldn't have a past that caught up with me. I might not like how this shit panned out because I feel like I needed to know why. At the same time, it doesn't even matter why the nigga did what he did. The fact remains the same. I'm still ahead of the Hernandez Cartel, my wife killed his bitch ass, and we're definitely getting married. All of the curve balls these people tried to throw at us we dodged the shit and came out stronger than ever. Who knew the day I took Princess from Lucifer that this would be life for me. She wasn't what a nigga like me went after. As a matter of fact, I didn't even look at her that way. I thank God we had drunk sex and created our son. My life would have no meaning today if we hadn't. It's funny how life comes full circle when you least expect it. I guess I was supposed to meet Princess and bring her home with me. In all honesty, she saved my life. Had it not been for her presence in my life, Humberto might have been successful in his hit on me. This story could have gone so many ways, but I'm glad it happened this way. It showed us how the life we live could change within the blink of an eye. It also shows you that blood doesn't mean shit, and they're more detrimental than an enemy could ever be. I'm good with the family I've created.

After showering and climbing into bed with her, I placed kisses on her face and lips. Her eyes instantly popped open for a minute we stared at each other before speaking a word.

"Are you mad at me?"

"I want to be, but I couldn't bring myself to. Tonight you defied me, but you did for your honor and for the sake of our family. Honestly, I wanted to be the one that pulled that trigger. I guess you killed my father, and I killed yours. We did what was best for one another. I know I'm a difficult nigga to love from time to time, but there is a method to my madness. Thank you for putting up with my wishy-washy ass behavior. I love you Princess, and don't you ever forget that shit."

"I love you too, Hercules. You've given me a life that I never thought I would have. This last year has been filled with ups and downs. There have been days where I felt like I wasn't what you really wanted. I used to lie awake on the east wing of the house and feel like a charity case. There I was pregnant living in a nigga's mansion with both of his baby mommas. I wanted to escape so bad, but I didn't because being in your house was better than being alone. With you, I had a family. The hardest thing in the world was living there and causing friction. Prior to me showing up, shit was cool with y'all. My presence in your life has caused so much drama. Through it all, you rode for me so hard. I fell in love with you the moment you chose me over someone you knew for years.

I love you so much, Hercules. I'm so sorry that my past keeps coming up and haunting us. I'm so embarrassed behind this Humberto situation, but I can't do anything to change the fact that it happened. My past doesn't define me. I used to think it did, but it doesn't. This life we're living isn't easy, but we do it with ease. I want to be your wife more today than I did yesterday. I'll always fight for you because you've always fought for me. Tonight was just me taking the necessary steps needed to secure our future. It wasn't about him threatening me about pictures or videos of me. It was about him trying to take everything I watch you work hard for day in and day out. He just kept talking, and I shot him. I will no longer stand back and allow people to bring harm to this family. We're getting married Saturday, and we will have a happily ever after. If I have to kill a couple of more motherfuckers, I would. I'm no longer allowing anyone to dictate my future. My future is with you and our kids. I'm just so excited to walk down the aisle and take your last name."

"Get up and get dressed right now!" Just hearing her say that shit let me know I couldn't wait.

"Where we going?"

"To find a Justice of the Peace. I'm marrying your pretty ass tonight."

"Noooo, Herc! My dress is too pretty. We can't keep doing this."

"Fuck that dress. Throw on some hood shit. We about to tie this knot ghetto as fuck!"

Princess quickly jumped out of bed, and we both got dressed and went to find an all-night chapel. That shit wasn't hard to find. After all, we were in Vegas, and them shits were on every corner. I couldn't wait any longer. We could have a big ass hood reception with the family and renew our vows with them. Right now at this moment, I was about to marry my soul mate. Fuck everything else! It was now or never. Since tomorrow isn't promised to anyone, we are doing this shit right now. If we don't do it right now it seems like there will be something else that comes up. I'm not willing to deal with no more bullshit while not being her husband. Whatever we go through going forward we will do it as husband and wife.

EPILOGUE: PRINCESS

I look back on my life and realize just how fortunate I am. Lying pool-side watching Zyion, Brittani, Baby Herc, and Sophia splash around in the pool with Hercules is everything. Not to mention Bonnie and Clyde running around and enjoying themselves. I still can't believe I live in a house with monkeys but I love it. I have everything I've ever wanted right in front of me. I'm six months pregnant with baby number three, and I'm more excited than ever to meet my second son. That night Hercules decided to get married on a whim he fucked me so good he dropped another seed off in me.

Looking at my husband and our kids enjoying the fruits of his labor makes me so grateful to be his wife and the mother of his children. The big wedding I dreamed of never happened because Hercules wanted to get that shit done and over with. At first, I wasn't really happy about the rushing, but now I'm extremely grateful. I love Hercules more than anything in this world. He's given me the best of everything. Outside of our kids, he has given me an extended family that loves me like I'm blood. It's like we're one big happy extended family.

Miami is the best friend that a girl could ever have. From the moment she met me, she accepted me. Miami gave me the game straight out the gate without hesitation. She's never switched up on me, and for that, I love her. Just watching how much her life has evolved since making things official with Diego is everything. She gave birth to a baby girl, and now she and Diego are planning their wedding. You ever looked at someone and wanted them to have all the happiness in the world? That's how I look at Miami. She's one of the realest bitches out here, and she deserves the world. I'm so happy she got that in Diego. That man loves her, Brittani, and their son Diego Jr. with everything inside of him.

I finally can say I have a mother who loves me more than life itself. There was a time where I hated Queenie and wished death upon her. Now, I love having her around, and we have so much fun together. She's such a boss these days. Hercules gave us a second chance at having a mother-daughter relationship. A lot of people would look at what I've been through because of Queenie. They will never understand why I choose to forgive her. I had to in order to move forward. That added with knowing what she had been through. Knowing that Queenie has gone above and beyond to make things right with us means everything. She's a wonderful grandmother. That lady goes above and beyond for her grandkids. She may have never been a good mother to me growing up, but she's the best grandmother our kids could ever have.

Passion and Gustavo are just being themselves and dealing with their bipolar relationship. Besides that, I'm still on a high knowing that I have a blood sister to share my life. I grew up as an only child and dreamed of having a sibling, so finding her has made my heart whole. I couldn't ask for a better sister to have. I can't wait for the day she has a family of her own but for now she's living her best life. She's young and rich as fuck. The world is her oyster and she can do whatever the fuck she wants no matter the cost.

Being Mrs. Hercules Hernandez is everything, but being my own boss is even better. After passing my GED test, I decided to buy a building and convert it into a woman's shelter. The shelter is geared towards women and their children who are victims of human trafficking. I used the money that Benito gave to me to invest in Sophia's House. I named it after my daughter because it was fitting. She was a product of evil, but an angel that had brought life into our family.

My nonprofit organization is the most important thing to me in this world outside of my family. I've come a long way, and I was one of the lucky ones who made it out. A lot of women don't get the same happily ever after as I have. My goal is to give back and give other victims a chance at a better life. Just having a second chance at living my best life makes me so thankful. Hercules could have been with any woman in this world, but he chose me. I'm a living witness that you can overcome anything. People will place obstacles in front of you, and all you have to do is knock them bitches down no matter what. I have a husband who loves me. Even though it took time for us to get to our happy place, we made it. Imagine that. I grew up not knowing love or ever knowing what it was like to have a hug. Now I'm Princess Delgado-Hernandez, and I'm married to the Plug!

The End

SUBSCRIBE

Text Shan to 22828 to stay up to date with new releases, sneak peeks, contest, and more....

SUBMISSIONS

To submit your manuscript to Shan Presents, please send the first three chapters and synopsis to submissions@shanpresents.com

CPSIA information can be obtained
at www.ICGtesting.com
Printed in the USA
LVHW092344251019
635428LV00001B/80/P

9 781096 250555